Phantom Tale

A Novella

By: Dylan Gibbs

Copyright © 2025 by Dylan Gibbs

All rights reserved.

This is a work of fiction. Names, characters, places, and incidents either are the product of the author's imagination or are used fictitiously, and any resemblance to actual persons, living or dead, business establishments, products, events, or locales is entirely coincidental.

For J.J.

ONE

Barry stared at the circular clock on the wall. He watched the second hand creep along. Each tick brought him closer to quitting time, but not quickly enough.

It was 3:25pm, and the bank was open another 35 minutes. It felt like an eternity. One of those days that just drags on and on.

Barry's feet were aching. They always did toward the end of his shift.

Would it kill them to buy a stool?

He shifted his weight from his left leg to his right as he heard a jingle from across the room. A little bell hung over the front door announcing each customer as they entered the building.

Barry sighed. It was Mrs. Crossman, a notorious pain in the ass. She was heading straight for Barry's counter even though there were several other tellers closer. Just his luck.

She waved a twenty dollar bill out in front of her as she collided with the counter.

"I need change," she screeched.

"Yes, Mrs. Crossman. How would you like the bills?" he asked, taking the twenty.

"However. Just make it snappy!"

Barry fished two fives and ten ones from the drawer. He counted the bills out in front of her and placed it in the palm of her wrinkled hand. She clenched her fist around the money and charged across the lobby to Mr. Meyers' office, Barry's boss.

She came out of the office a moment later with a satisfied smile on her face.

"Hey, Barry. Can I see you a moment?" Mr. Meyers called from behind his desk.

Barry blew out air slowly from his lungs and made his way across the lobby.

"Close the door behind you," Mr. Meyers told him as he entered the office.

Barry did.

"So, what's the deal, Barry? Mrs. Crossman said you gave her an attitude."

Barry cracked his first real smile of the day. "Attitude?"

"Yeah, Barry. We need to create an inviting atmosphere here at LockKey Bank. We always treat our customers with respect."

"Yeah, I know. I don't know why she would have..."

He cut him off. "I'm not looking for excuses. Remember that the customer is always right."

Barry could feel his temper starting to flare.

"Well, Peter, this particular customer wasn't right. In fact, I think you already know that. I think you're well aware she's an old hag that likes to make trouble each and every time she steps foot inside the building."

"You'll address me as Mr. Meyers. And I'm well aware she can be a handful. That doesn't give you a right to be rude to her."

"I WASN'T," he shouted.

"Another outburst like that and you'll be finding another job. Get back to your desk. This conversation is over."

Barry swung the office door open and marched back to his spot behind the counter. He glanced at the clock.

It read 3:29pm.

"There's no fucking way," he muttered.

Barry lowered his head down on the countertop and groaned loudly.

A short time later, Barry drove through the heart of his small town, Orchard Bay, in Upstate New York.

His black tie had been cast into the passenger seat of his old, beat-up pickup truck. The sound of his rust chewed muffler could be heard three streets over.

Barry tossed a ketchup smeared wrapper into a crumpled fast-food bag and cracked the window open.

He was on his way to see his therapist. Or counselor. Barry wasn't sure which title she had or what made those two professions any different. He just knew she couldn't prescribe him anything. If his therapist felt he needed to be on something, which he wasn't, she would make the suggestion to Barry's medical doctor. That's who had sent him there in the first place.

He pulled onto West Street and eased the truck to the curb. Barry, a twenty-eight-year-old man in a plaid button-up shirt and blue jeans, climbed out of the cab.

He was five foot eleven but if anyone asked, he always said he was six foot even. His unused online dating profile said six foot one.

Barry had shaggy brown hair, a naturally muscular build, and a faint dimple on each of his cheeks.

He approached the white two-story house and pulled open the front door.

"Hey, Darcy," he said, shuffling inside.

A chubby, middle-aged woman looked up from the desk. She was folding a wrapper over a half-eaten chocolate bar.

Barry wasn't sure why, but her mouth reminded him of a dinosaur. Maybe it was from the television show he watched as a child. It had that baby dinosaur that yelled "not the mama." It looked quite similar to that.

"Hey, Barry. Miss Perkins is still with a client. You can have a seat in the waiting room. I'll call you when she's ready," she told him.

Barry nodded and entered the waiting room on the right. He was surprised to see a young lady already seated inside. He rarely saw anyone else waiting to be seen, let alone someone younger than himself.

She looked up at him with big doe-like blue eyes. She didn't smile, just watched him as he took a seat.

Barry couldn't help but take the young lady in. She was quite pretty. She had golden shoulder-length hair. It was parted in the center with bangs long enough to get into her eyes.

She wore an oversized green knit sweater that fell to one side, exposing a bare shoulder.

He realized he was staring and looked down at the floor. She was wearing Chuck Taylors, high tops. This chick definitely had style.

"I'm Kate," she said.

Barry looked up.

"Barry. Nice to meet you."

"What are you in for, Barry?"

She was direct. No playing around.

"I was a little too honest with my doctor," he admitted.

"How do you mean?"

"Uh... We were talking and I may have mentioned that I wanted to step in front of a runaway train."

"Yup. That'll do it," she said with a hint of a smile blooming.

"What about you?" he asked.

"Oh, I'm here because I'm... strange."

Barry smiled. "How do you mean?"

"I bite people."

Barry burst out laughing. He had been taken off guard. She had to be twenty-one or twenty-two-years-old and a whole five foot five. Picturing this cute little nugget of a human on the attack was such a funny image.

"Sorry, I don't mean to laugh. You bite people, you say?"

"Yeah. I mean, not everyone. It's not like I run around all day biting folks. It's just when I get angry. I jump at them and chomp down."

She made an exaggerated biting motion with her mouth.

Barry laughed harder. So hard that little tears were forming at the corner of his eyes.

Kate was studying him with a grin on her face.

"I can't tell if you're joking or not," he told her.

She shrugged.

"Barry, Miss Perkins will see you now," Darcy bellowed from the next room. "Kate, give Mr. Williams another five minutes please."

"Looks like I'm up," Barry said, getting to his feet.

He moved toward the door then abruptly stopped and turned back to Kate.

"Any chance I could get your number?" he asked.

Kate smiled wide enough to expose the rows of perfectly straight, white teeth. She dug into her purse, pulled out a business card and jotted her number on the back. She handed it to Barry.

He looked at the card. It was for a tattoo shop in the city, Sunset Tattoo. He'd heard of the place but had never been there. He flipped it over to see her bubbly handwriting on the back.

"I'll give you a call," he said.

"Sure thing."

Barry made his way up the staircase to Miss Perkins' office. She stood up from an upholstered chair as he entered the room.

"Barry, come on in. Have a seat or lay down. Whichever you think will be more comfortable."

"Thanks, Lucy," he said, taking a seat on the leather couch.

"So, last time you were here we were making a little headway, and you stormed out. Do you feel like talking about..."

"Not today," he interrupted.

"Ok. So how would you like to start?"

"I've been thinking a lot about my childhood lately. I don't know if it's the whole innocence of childhood or what exactly, but I felt more connected to everything, you know?'

"Can you elaborate?"

"Just the act of stepping outside as a kid was different. The smell of fresh cut grass. The gentle motion of the trees in the wind. I'd watch clouds float by, and I'd feel connected to it all somehow. It felt like the world belonged to me and I belonged to it. I was a part of nature. It's hard to put the feeling into words. I was happy."

"What is it like for you now?"

"I don't feel anything. It's just one shitty, unspecial day after another."

"We'd describe that as melancholy. It is an all-too-common feeling with a lot of adults. Can I ask you the last time you remember feeling happy or excited?" she asked.

Barry chuckled. "In your waiting room about ten minutes ago."

Lucy's head tilted in surprise.

"Tell me about that."

"I met a young lady down there. I was quite smitten with her right away. I grabbed her number," Barry said holding the business card up for her to see.

"Is she a client here?"

"She's seeing Alan Williams I guess."

"Barry, I don't think it's a great idea to begin a relationship with anyone while you're in your current state of mind. It's best to work on yourself, get healthy, then pursue someone. It's a particularly bad idea to date someone else with mental difficulties. It could really hurt you both in the long run."

"Hey, I didn't say I was going to marry her. I just met her. Maybe we'll just be friends. It's all right to have friends, isn't it?"

Lucy paused for a moment.

"What exactly drew you to this person?"

"I don't know. I was pretty amused when she told me she bites people."

Lucy Perkins raised her hand to her head and began rubbing her temple.

Barry had returned home after his appointment. He lived in a cramped apartment overtop of a barber shop downtown. It wasn't his ideal place to stay but it fit his budget.

He sank into a well-worn recliner and zoned into his guilty pleasure, reality television. He stayed there well into the night.

He was dreading the next morning as usual. Eight long hours at his mundane job at the bank sounded like absolute torture.

Had he known what was actually in store for him the following day, perhaps he would have got more sleep.

TWO

Barry woke the next morning still in his recliner. His phone sat on the end table next to him blaring a heavy metal song that he hated. It was pretty much the only thing that could rouse him from slumber.

Barry tapped the little red circle labeled "stop" and was plunged into silence. He closed the legs on the chair and rose to his feet.

He stared at the coffee maker, contemplating whether to brew a cup or stop for something tastier on his way to work. He opted for the latter.

After a steaming hot shower, Barry threw on a polo shirt and khaki pants. On Fridays Mr. Meyers allowed them to dress without a tie.

He grabbed a light jacket from the back of a chair and ran down the stairs to the street.

The morning was unusually quiet. There were no mourning doves permeating the break of day with their call. The dog down the street wasn't barking incessantly. All was calm.

Barry hardly took notice of any of that though as he rushed to his little red pickup truck and turned his key. The truck roared to life and Barry drove straight through town to his favorite coffee shop, Brew Haven.

When he arrived, Barry circled around to the drive-thru speaker and waited. His eyes flicked from the clock on the dashboard to the speaker box on the menu board. He loudly cleared his throat. There was no response.

Barry's patience thinned and he pulled his truck around to the front entrance. Immediately as he entered the cafe, he could tell the place was closed. There was no delicious scent of roasting coffee beans floating through the air to greet him. The lights were off behind the counter.

That's strange. Why was the door unlocked if they're closed?

"Hello?" Barry shouted.

There was no reply.

Barry got back into his truck and continued the short drive to the bank.

As he drove, he became aware of how quiet the morning really was. There was no other traffic. No one was out jogging or walking their dogs. The town seemed to be completely empty.

Barry pulled into the parking lot of LockKey Bank. There were several cars parked in the lot but none of them he recognized as belonging to his coworkers. Perhaps the green minivan belonged to Rachel, she was a young mother, and he had no clue what she drove.

Barry jogged to the side door and pulled it open.

Inside the lights were still off and the place was silent.

"Hello," Barry called. "Is anyone here?"

There was no response.

Barry opened the few office doors and checked the break room. They were all empty. As he searched around the building, the clock struck 8am. The bank was officially open for business at 8am. There was no fathomable way the entire staff was late for work. Something was going on.

Barry pulled out his cell phone and typed in "Orchard Bay NY" in the search. That only brought up a list of businesses and activities in the area.

Barry cleared the search bar and wrote "Emergency Orchard Bay NY." It only brought up a list of emergency services and an article talking about the flood in the area seven years prior.

At 8:32am, Barry decided no one was going to show up and exited the building. When he stepped out into the breeze, he scanned his surroundings. There was not one person in sight.

Should I start knocking on doors? I'll look crazy as hell when someone answers.

Barry considered his predicament a moment. Where was there a public space he could travel to that he would surely find people?

The mall.

It didn't open until 9am but the place was always packed. Plus, it's right in the middle of a city. There should be people everywhere. Maybe someone would know why Orchard Bay was a complete ghost town.

Barry fired up the old pickup truck and made his way to the highway. His eyes darted from the road ahead of him to the opposing lanes of traffic across the median. There was not a single vehicle in sight.

Barry felt a tightening in his chest. His pulse quickened. His breathing became labored. He considered pulling off to the side of the road but instead he cracked his window and tried to calm his breathing. He took slow deliberate breaths until he felt like himself again.

Why is this happening to me? Where the hell did everyone go?

Barry took the next exit and drove into the heart of the city. His fears were confirmed. The city was empty.

Vehicles lined the streets. The traffic lights continued to go from red to green. Digital billboards still advertised their products, but there were no signs of people anywhere.

Barry pulled into the massive parking lot that surrounded the shopping mall. Cars freckled the spaces around him.

He didn't bother parking in a spot. Instead, he pulled his truck right up to one of the many entrance doors and got out. He could hear music playing lightly over the mall's overhead speakers. Perhaps that should have been a good sign, but Barry had already lost all hope of seeing another living person.

Barry yanked on the door, half expecting it to be locked, but it opened easily in his hand. He stepped inside the building and looked around.

Barry had visited the mall many times throughout his youth. The waxed floor and grey walls displaying 90's style art was a familiar sight and helped calm his nerves. But still, there wasn't a soul in sight.

Barry cupped his hands around his mouth and yelled, "Hello. Is anybody in here?"

He heard his voice echo down the empty halls.

I'm dead. I died in my sleep.

He stood there a moment longer.

No, couldn't be. I'm not dead. This is a dream. It's nothing more than a vivid dream. I just need to wake myself up.

Barry impulsively ran to the first bodega that sat in the center of the hallway. He slammed his fist down onto the glass case that was displaying cheap watches. It shattered. Most of the glass fell into the display case. A few shards landed amongst Barry's shoes.

Barry reached down and selected a large chunk of broken glass. He held it to his wrist, paused for a moment, and then dragged it across.

The pain was immediate. Blood flowed from the wound, ran down Barry's arm and dripped from his elbow to the waxed floor.

Barry you stupid asshole! This isn't a dream!

He yanked off his shirt and applied it to the cut.

I'm alive. So, what the hell could be happening? Was there a rapture? Am I a sinner, and the only one that wasn't taken? No. That doesn't add up. I'm not that bad of a guy. It's got to be something else. What though?

Barry checked the wound on his wrist. The blood had already stopped. He hadn't cut himself deep enough to do any kind of real damage.

Barry tossed the blood-stained polo shirt into the trash can and walked to the first store that sold men's apparel. He found a graphic t-shirt he liked and checked for an xl. There was one left on the bottom of the pile. Barry pulled it on and removed the sticker.

It's not really stealing if I'm the last person on Earth, right?

Barry naturally gravitated over to the movie theater. He loved films, especially thrillers. There was a fantastic new one out but now Barry would never see it.

Unless...

Barry made his way over to the concession stand and hopped over the counter. It took a minute to figure out how it worked but there was a tablet behind the counter that listed each movie with set times. You could override the times with the push of a button and play them anytime you wish.

Barry laughed to himself.

Maybe having the world to myself won't be such a terrible thing.

Barry studied the popcorn machine and flipped a heating switch. He began ransacking the cupboards underneath to find the corn kernels when suddenly he heard a sound in the distance.

Barry sat down on the counter and swung his legs back over to the other side. He slowly walked out of the theater into the mall, trying to focus on the sound. It almost sounded like someone dragging chains. Heavy metal chains.

That meant someone was alive beside Barry. He rushed down the hallway toward the sound when it abruptly went quiet again. Barry broke into a desperate run, trying to get as close to where he thought the sound had come from as possible.

"Hey! Is anyone else here?" Barry shouted.

There was no reply.

Barry searched for a bit longer but eventually gave up. Perhaps it was only his mind playing tricks on him.

As he was making his way back to the theater, he noticed that the overhead doors for each store opened and closed with a thin metal chain. Barry approached one and gave it a push. Not quite the sound he had heard but it was close enough to put him at ease. Perhaps the ventilation system kicked on and blew one of the chains around.

Regardless, Barry returned to the theater and located the kernels. He filled the machine and popped way too much corn for one person. Barry took a moment to put his nose over the holding bin and inhaled deeply. Something about the smell of fresh popcorn always transported him back to childhood.

He grabbed one of the giant cups promoting a kid's movie and filled it with cola. He went back to the tablet and pressed play for screen one.

Barry rushed over to the first theater to see that it had worked. The movie was cycling through all its pre-movie ads as he took a seat in the center of the room.

Barry spent the entire day there watching movie after movie. He made hotdogs on the rollers and pretzels in the toaster oven. Although he constantly felt like he was doing something wrong and he'd be caught at any moment, nothing of the sort happened. He simply had a lovely day.

When it grew late and Barry felt himself getting tired, he approached the exit door. Night had fallen, and the parking lot lights had automatically come up. Normally he'd see little swarms of bugs hovering around each lamp. Not that night. He hadn't seen a bug all day. Nor had he spotted a bird, a stray cat, or even a squirrel.

The anxious feeling returned and suddenly Barry didn't want to go outside. He would spend the night right there in the mall.

The entire world belongs to me now. I guess I can sleep wherever I wish.

Barry located a mattress store next to the entrance where he had parked his truck. A few of the mattresses inside had been made up with sheets and comforters for display. A perfect spot for Barry to rest his head for the night.

He lifted a floral comforter and slid underneath. The bed was surprisingly comfortable and the light music playing overhead in the mall seemed to lull him into a deep sleep.

"Sir! Sir! What the hell are you doing?"

Barry's eyes burst open. He was looking at a chubby mall security guard with a square badge pinned to his white shirt.

"I was uhm... testing out this mattress and I must have dozed off," Barry lied.

"The mall doesn't open for another hour. How did you get in here?" the guard asked.

Barry climbed out of the display bed.

"Where was everyone yesterday?" Barry asked.

"Everyone who? The employees?"

The guard looked toward two women wearing matching shirts labeled "Mattress World." They had probably been the ones that called security. They looked terrified of Barry.

"I mean everyone. The whole city was empty Friday," said Barry.

"Sir, today is Friday. Are you all right? Did you do any drugs?" the guard asked.

Barry pulled out his cellphone. It was Friday... again. He pushed past the guy and ran out of the store. There were dozens of people walking through the halls. He could hear the guard's radio squawk behind him and Barry ran for his truck.

He could faintly hear the security guard say, "Get that plate number."

Barry climbed inside the pickup and tore out of the parking lot.

What the hell happened? Was yesterday real? Did I dream the whole thing?

Barry flipped his arm over, exposing the jagged cut across his wrist. It was fresh, a day old.

No. That definitely wasn't a dream.

THREE

Barry merged his truck into heavy traffic. The highway was maddeningly busy on weekday mornings, and this was no exception.

What the hell happened to me? I couldn't have been sleepwalking, I drove there! Plus, everything would have been locked up that late at night. How would I have even gotten inside the building? None of this makes any sense. It's like I lived a day that never happened. It's Friday all over again.

Barry's eyes lit up. The clock on the dashboard read 8:11am. Barry slammed his palm against the steering wheel.

"Damn it!"

Barry kept an eye on the road and maneuvered his cellphone out of his pants pocket. He dialed a number with his thumb and raised the phone to his ear.

"LockKey Bank, this is Mr. Meyers."

"Hey, it's Barry. I was..."

Meyers cut him off. "Do you own a clock? Look at the damn time Barry. You've been on thin ice all week. Now you're going to be late on top of it all?"

"I've been sick," Barry lied. "I was trying to get to the phone, to call in, but I kept throwing up again and again."

"All right. All right. I don't need the details. You know this is your second call off this year, right? That's two points."

"I understand."

Barry waited for another comment from his boss, but the phone was quiet. Barry lifted it away from his face and looked at the screen. The call had already been ended.

What an asshole.

Barry pulled off at the Orchard Bay exit and drove through his hometown. People were standing on Main Street chatting. Folks were jogging and walking their dogs. The town was a bustling metropolis compared to the day before.

What Barry really took notice of was the noise. The morning was so much louder with the vehicles, lawn mowers, people, and animals. Especially the birds. Of course, the sound of his obnoxiously loud exhaust drowned out most of it as he pulled into the parking space outside the barbershop.

He climbed the stairs to his apartment and threw his keys on the counter. He showered and dressed for the early start to his weekend. He had felt a little guilt for calling into work; however, he needed to sort himself out. The bank could get by one day without him.

Barry couldn't shake the events of the previous day out of his head, so he decided to act. He pulled out his phone, plopped into his favorite recliner, and dialed the number for his therapist.

It rang repeatedly, then connected to an answering machine.

"Hey, it's Barry Abrams. I was hoping to make an emergency appointment today with Lucy Perkins. I don't know if she has an available slot, but I need to see her before my normal Monday appointment. Thank you."

Barry closed out the call and leaned back in the chair. The business card with bubbly numbers scrawled on the back sat on the table next to him. Barry picked up the card and took a deep breath.

I need to talk to someone about what happened yesterday. I don't want to freak this poor girl out though.

He sat for a moment, considering his options, and then punched the digits into his phone. He heard two rings and then the sound of Kate's voice.

"Hello?" she answered, the word heavy with sleep.

"Oh, I'm sorry. I forgot how early it was. I didn't mean to wake you," said Barry.

"Who is this?" she asked with a tinge of amusement in her voice.

"This is Barry. We met two days ago at the therapist's office."

She laughed. "That was last night. I'm happy to hear from you though."

Barry slapped his forehead.

"Oh, right. It was a long day. Anyway, do you think you'd like to go get a coffee later and chat?"

"Sure, after a bit more sleep. I get moody if I don't get at least fourteen hours."

"What? Fourteen hours? Are you joking?"

Kate laughed. "Text me the address. I'll meet you at two."

"Sounds great. I'll see you then."

"Ciao."

Barry hung up and smiled from ear to ear.

God her laugh is great.

Barry hadn't been out on a date in over a year. He was nervous but excited at the same time.

Wait, is it a date? I never said it was a date. Does she think it's a date?

Barry sat at one of the outdoor tables at Brew Haven. His leg bounced nervously as he waited for Kate to show. He had arrived twenty minutes early and checked the time on his phone roughly every thirty seconds.

At exactly 2pm, a bright yellow Volkswagen Beetle pulled into the parking lot. Kate climbed out of the driver's seat. Her golden hair was braided into two short pigtails. She wore a brown skirt and a dark green sweater that showed her midriff.

She spotted Barry and approached him with a smile.

"Hey, how are you?" Barry asked, getting to his feet.

"I'm great," said Kate.

She came up to him and gave him a light hug.

"Shall we?" Barry asked, pointing to the counter inside.

They ordered coffee and a couple of pastries. Barry held the door, and they made their way back outside to the table.

They made small talk at first and then shared some major life experiences. Kate still lived with her parents.

They had renovated their garage so she could have her own space. She worked part-time at a record shop in Arlington. That was the nearby city that housed the Arlington Mall that Barry had woken up in that very morning.

New York is full of towns that are named after bigger cities or countries. Paris, New York. Mexico, New York. Even Syracuse is the English version of Siracusa, the city in Italy. Arlington, New York, was no different, a cheap version of a bigger and better city.

Barry went on to tell her how his folks had divorced when he was fresh out of high school. His father moved across the country and his mother remarried less than a year later. Naturally, Barry didn't get along with his new stepfather, and he was forced to move into the small apartment above the barbershop before he was ready to strike out on his own.

Barry found Kate easy to talk to. She cracked a lot of jokes, and the conversation never ran dry. It turned out they both loved cryptids and briefly talked about Bigfoot and Mothman.

"Can I completely derail the conversation and tell you about the strangest thing that ever happened to me?" Barry asked. "I need to tell somebody."

"Oh, yeah. I have a feeling I'm going to love this."

"This is my second Friday."

Kate grinned. "Already lost me."

Barry laughed then grew serious. "Yesterday I woke up and everyone was gone. It was an empty world. No animals. No people. Just me."

Kate's eyes narrowed. "Oh, yeah? What did you do all day?"

"Well, I figured I should go look for other people. At first, I thought everyone may have been evacuated due to an emergency or I missed some huge event. I couldn't find anything online. So, I trekked off to Arlington and went to the mall. I figured there had to be someone there."

"Was there?"

"Not a soul. So, I decided to enjoy a few movies at the theater. I'm almost ashamed to admit I watched four in a row. Lots of pretzel bites and roller hot dogs too."

"So, what was this? A vivid dream or something" Kate asked.

"That's what I thought at first too, but no. I tried to wake myself up," he said, lifting his wrist so she could see the gash across his wrist.

"Jesus, Barry. You're serious?"

"Kate, I don't know how to explain it because I still don't understand what happened. I went to sleep in the mattress store, as one does in that situation, and I woke up with security in my face. Everything was back to normal. People were everywhere and it was Friday all over again."

"You must have been sleepwalking. You just didn't wake up when you cut yourself."

"I drove there."

"People can drive in that state. I've heard of that happening before," Kate told him.

"I can remember each of the movies I watched. I can tell you the whole plot of each. Plus, how'd I get inside the mall? How did I get inside the mattress store after hours for that matter?"

"Have you called your therapist?" she asked tentatively.

Barry laughed. "Yeah, I'd think I was crazy too. The first thing I did when I got home was call. I got the voicemail and left a message."

"I don't think you're crazy. We met at a therapist's office though. I'm sure we are both a little skeptical of each other," she said with a laugh.

"Yeah, heck of a thing to bring up on a first date, huh? Probably should have kept it to myself."

"No, I'm glad you told me. I'm invested now," she told him.

Kate smiled and downed the last of her coffee. She gathered her garbage and threw it in the bin by the door. Barry walked her over to her car.

"I'll give you a call then?" Barry asked.

"If you don't hear from me first."

That evening, Barry cooked himself a TV dinner and had a quiet night at home. He had planned on staying up late watching old monster movies, but he grew tired earlier than usual.

He brushed his teeth and crawled into bed. The floral scent of the freshly washed sheets filled his nose as he pulled the comforter up to his chin. Barry had his window cracked open and he drifted off listening to the steady thrum of cars passing by on the street below.

When the early morning light poured in through the window shades and reached Barry's bed, his eyes fluttered open. The first thing he noticed was the absolute silence of the world around him.

FOUR

Barry tossed the covers off the side of the bed and rose to his feet.

No. No. No. This can't be happening again.

He yanked on the drawstring and sent the window shades up with a loud clack. Barry hoisted the window the rest of the way open and stuck his head outside.

No cars passed by. No pedestrians on the sidewalks. Not even a bird chirping in a nearby tree.

Barry snatched his phone from the charger and dialed Kate's number.

Come on. Come on. Pick up.

No voicemail picked up, just endless ringing.

Barry hung up and dialed 911.

Desperate times call for desperate measures.

Again, no voicemail, no answering machine, and definitely no emergency dispatch.

Barry sat back down on the corner of the bed. His heart pounded away in his chest.

"Okay, so I slept and everyone disappeared. Then I slept and everyone came back. Then I slept, and everyone disappeared again. Obviously, the answer is to go back to bed. It's clearly a pattern," Barry told the empty room.

He laid back down and folded a single white bedsheet over himself. He positioned his head on the feather pillow and squeezed his eyes shut. He still felt his heart jackhammer away beneath his ribcage. His minded flooded with questions and dozens of crazy possibilities of what could be occurring.

His eyes burst back open.

"How the hell am I supposed to sleep at a time like this?" he yelled.

Barry dressed for the day and snagged his keys off the counter.

I've got an idea.

He climbed into his pickup and floored it. The vehicle shot through Orchard Bay at reckless speeds, straight to LockKey Bank. Barry drove over the curb and parked right on the sidewalk. He hopped out and stormed his way to the front entrance. The door was unlocked, and the lights were off. Barry cautiously entered and made his way to his boss's office.

Barry flipped on the light. Two framed photos sat on the desk. Peter Meyers on a white sandy beach with his wife. Then a photo of an older couple that Barry didn't recognize. It may have been Peter's parents.

Barry pulled open the top drawer. Nestled beside a stack of paperwork was a little black box with four round dials. He had seen Mr. Meyers put in the code dozens of times. Barry twisted each dial to the desired number and heard a small click. He lifted the lid to the lockbox and retrieved a key labeled "Vault."

Next, Barry took a letter opener from the desk and made his way out to the main lobby. Behind counter number one was a small red button with a keyhole beside it. Barry stuck the little brass key into the hole and twisted. The red button lit up. Barry held the button down and then jammed the letter opener in the space between the button and its housing. It remained depressed.

Barry smiled and circled around to the back hallway. A huge metal vault loomed before him. There was a metal wheel, much like a vehicle's steering wheel, mounted to the center of the vault. Barry took it in his hand and spun until he heard the latch give and the vault door pop open.

Barry pulled the massively thick door on its hinges and revealed tables and tables of sorted money.

Just a little experiment. I won't be greedy.

Barry lifted two large bundles of cash from the first table. They were each wrapped tightly with a slip of paper that read "$10,000."

Barry resecured the vault door, ducked back out to the lobby, plucked the letter opener out and removed the key.

He went back into his boss's office and replaced the items, making sure that everything looked the same as when he had first arrived.

Barry smiled and stuffed one of the bundles of bills into the pocket of a rain jacket that Peter Meyers kept hung up in the corner of his office. The other bundle Barry took with him and threw it into his truck's glove compartment.

Let's see if you're still there tomorrow.

Barry started up the truck and said to himself, "Guess I'm off to the mall again. There's a couple of movies I haven't got to yet."

He set course for the highway and the Arlington Mall.

On the rooftop of Arlington's most luxurious hotel, a man wearing a beat-up, brown leather jacket lowered his binoculars. His black hair was streaked with gray and slicked back behind his ears. He wore a stern look on his face.

"God damn idiot!"

"What? Same guy?" asked a freckled-faced teenager behind him.

"Yeah. The truck is loud as hell and he's going back to the mall," said the older guy.

"Never go to the same place two days in a row. That's rule number one."

"I'm surprised they weren't drawn in yesterday by the sound of that exhaust."

"We going to go warn him?" the teen asked.

"Nah, he'll be dead before we can get there."

FIVE

This time when Barry pulled into the mall parking lot, he took a normal spot among the few other vehicles. He had no plans to spend the night inside the building, but if he did, he didn't want to wake up the next morning and draw unnecessary attention to himself like last time, parked up on the sidewalk.

Barry planned on keeping a tight eye on the time. He wanted to make sure he left while the sun was still up.

He couldn't put into words why exactly, but last time he was at the Arlington Mall and stared off into the dark parking lot, he couldn't bring himself to step outside. It was something primal that screamed inside himself not to walk out into the night.

Of course, the whole thing was silly. There wasn't a living soul around, not even an animal. What was there to be afraid of?

Barry climbed out of the small pickup. A cool breeze pushed his shirt flat against his chest. He closed his eyes and turned his face to the warm sun.

He couldn't recall the last time he had done that. Although being alone was frightening, something about a world void of people eased some of his anxiety.

Barry crossed the parking lot toward the front entrance to the mall and went inside. The loud click of the heavy door closing behind him echoed through the empty halls.

Barry had entered through the food court this time. He stopped and surveyed all the little restaurants that lined the sides of the room.

He could make a pizza and bring it into the theater with him. If it was anything like the last time, all the ingredients should be there.

The sub place would be even easier though. No cooking. No wait time. Just build a big heaping sandwich.

Barry scratched his chin, lost in indecision.

A darkness passed over the front doors and windows. Barry turned to look. Perhaps a rainstorm was coming on.

Something seemed off about it though. He leaned forward to study the darkening entrance.

It was as if a rain cloud had left the sky and was floating into the glass windows. This was no rain cloud though. It was much too dark. Too well formed. The oddity of it had Barry mesmerized.

Is that smoke? It's so black.

Tendrils of the black cloud seeped in through the cracks around the doors.

Barry was frozen in place, watching with great interest. His mind was struggling to make sense of what exactly he was watching unfold before him.

The smoke finished filtering in through the door and gathered just inside the building. It didn't spread like smoke though. It pooled together in a tight area.

He saw shapes forming. A bit of cloth seemed to whip through the heavy black cloud. Then something shiny protruded from the wall of smoke. It was definitely metal.

Barry took a step closer.

What the hell is that? How did metal just materialize out of smoke?

It wasn't just metal though. It was something sharp. A blade. Barry searched his mind for the name of the farm tool it resembled.

A scythe! Like the Grim Reaper carries!

Suddenly the cloud of smoke finished taking shape. It was humanoid and impossibly large. An 8-foot tall, cloaked creature stood at the mall entrance.

Barry could not see its face well under the hood it wore. He could just make out a skeletal structure of a bare skull with blood red eyes. There was no visible iris, nor pupil, but he could tell the creature was watching him closely.

It lurched forward. Its cloak dragged behind it as it moved at a steady pace straight for Barry.

Barry quickly found his feet and got moving. He ran between the rows of food court tables and slid into the long shopping mall hallway. He turned and watched the creature in pursuit behind him.

The creature wasn't fast, but it still moved at a fair pace. Barry heard no footsteps. The cloaked thing was as silent as the world around him.

Barry took off running down the long stretch of hall. His footfalls against the waxed floor echoed off the walls. He couldn't remember the last time he ran so hard. Probably in gym class his senior year of high school.

He had almost made it to the other end of the building when he risked another look back. The cloaked creature was still coming but Barry had outrun it by a good stretch.

He stood there for a moment fighting to catch his breath. He lifted his shirt up and breathed through the cloth, a little trick he had learned as a child to slow his breathing.

How long can I outrun this thing?

The hallway just ahead split into a large T. There were exits on both sides of the intersecting hall. The exit to the left had a huge black cloud pushing its way through the doors.

Fuck! You've got to be kidding me. There are two of these things?

Barry darted to the right and slammed through the large metal doors out into the parking lot. He was nowhere near his truck; it was on the complete other side of the damn mall.

"Over here!"

Barry scanned the lot for the voice. A young teenager was zipping toward him on one of those electronic bicycles.

What? Another person?

The teen wore a black Nirvana hoodie with a yellow smiley face on the front. He came to a stop in front of Barry.

"Get on."

Barry looked at the bike. How was he supposed to get on?

"The pegs. Put your feet on the pegs and hold on," the kid yelled.

Barry put his feet on the metal bars that protruded from center of the back wheel. He grabbed the teenager by the shoulders to steady himself.

The teen sent the bike forward, but Barry was concerned over the speed, or lack thereof. He leaned over to look at the little screen mounted to the handlebars. The bike was only going 16mph.

"What the hell, man. Does this thing go any faster?" Barry shouted.

The cloud of black smoke was seeping out of the mall into the parking lot.

"Calm down, dude. It does go faster when two people aren't on it. But we're going plenty fast to outrun reapers."

"Why wouldn't you grab a car or a motorcycle? We need to move faster."

"Nah, we're good. Those things make too much noise. Noise draws them to you. This bike is almost silent, just a little hum."

Barry turned to look. The reaper had taken shape and was moving through the lot as the bike hit the main road.

"Aren't they going to follow us?"

"Yeah, for a while. Once we get a bit further, I'll start making a bunch of turns. They'll lose us," the teen told him. "Just be thankful it was only reapers that found you."

"What do you mean? There are different creatures than just those... reapers?"

"Hell yeah. There are a ton of different phantoms here. The worst case would be a shrieker. They are the white ones, mostly translucent. They can't harm you themselves but they're fast and they follow you around screeching like a son of a bitch. It calls all the other phantoms right to you. You would have been toast if one of those had found you."

"Well, thankfully I had you here. Before I forget to say it, thank you for saving my ass."

The teen laughed. "No problem. But just to be clear, if I had heard a shrieker in the mall, I would have jetted."

"Yeah, that's fair. I'm Barry by the way. Barry Abrams."

"Good to meet you, Barry. I'm Owen."

"I didn't know anyone else was alive in this world... place... void... whatever it is."

"Yeah, it's me and my buddy, Johnny. He's pissed I came to rescue you though, so we won't be meeting up with him at all today. He said if I led one of those things back to him, he'd kill me before the phantom had a chance."

"Sounds like a great guy," said Barry.

Owen laughed. "He's not so bad. Overly cautious. His circumstances are a bit different than you or I."

"Yeah, how so?"

"Eh, that's his story to tell. We can catch him at the clock tower tomorrow morning. That's where we're meeting up," said Owen. "Hold on tight. Here comes the fun part."

Owen turned sharply off the main road onto a residential street with green front lawns and neat rows of well-kept houses. Barry clutched Owen's shoulders, trying not to fall from the little pegs. He could feel his foot slipping. Owen quickly turned down another street, then another.

They gained considerable speed coasting down a steep hill and took a blind corner around a delivery van.

Owen yelled, "Oh fuck!"

Barry couldn't see what had startled the boy. He was too busy tumbling off the electric bicycle after the abrupt stop.

Barry smashed the side of his head off the trunk of a parked car. After that, everything went black.

SIX

Barry woke on hard ground. It didn't have the rough feel of road; the texture was too smooth. His eyes fluttered open but he still couldn't tell where he was.

He squinted and tried his best to make out his surroundings in the dim light. There were stacks of cardboard boxes, old furniture, and what looked like a water heater.

Somehow, he had ended up in a basement.

Barry sat up. His head screamed with pain. He raised his hand and felt the crust of dried blood in his hair. It didn't seem like much. His head was swimming though, so he laid back down against the concrete. His head rested against something soft. A balled up black hooded sweatshirt. The one Owen had been wearing.

Did that kid drag me down here?

Barry heard the patter of feet across the length of the ceiling. A child, maybe two. Then the hard heavy footsteps of an adult.

Shit. I'm in someone's house and I'm not in the phantom realm anymore. I can't let the family find me down here. How the hell would I explain this to a police officer?

Barry got slowly to his feet. There were two flights of stairs. A long set that clearly led into the house and then a short set that led to a pair of oversized metal doors.

He scooped the sweatshirt off the floor and slowly opened one of the large metal doors. The hinges were rusted, and the door made a loud squeal as it opened. Barry cringed, raising his shoulders to his ears.

He stayed perfectly still in the bright light of the morning, listening for any indication that he'd been discovered. All was quiet.

Barry stepped onto the grass and slowly lowered the door behind him. He ducked low to the ground and rushed past the windows, getting to the sidewalk as quickly as he could.

He pulled his phone from his front pocket. Thankfully, it had survived his fall from the bike. The front screen showed that it was Saturday, 10:03am.

Barry looked at his surroundings. He didn't recognize the neighborhood and wasn't sure which direction the mall was located. He had to get back there though. That's where his truck was parked.

He typed in the Arlington Mall into the search bar, clicked the button for directions, then clicked on the little picture of the guy walking.

3.2 miles. Did we really travel that far on that bike? Guess that thing can move after all.

Barry's head was pounding, and it was a good possibility he'd turn some heads walking around with dried blood caked in his hair, but he had to get moving. He was not excited about the journey, but hell, what *was* he excited about these days?

He straightened out his wrinkled clothing the best that he could, trying to look presentable. Then he began to walk.

When Barry arrived back at his apartment, the first thing he did was climb into the steaming hot shower. He scrubbed his hair clean of the blood and watched as the reddened water and dried flakes circled the drain. The tiny red pieces reminded Barry of peeled paint.

After cracking the bathroom window and airing out the steam, Barry assessed his head in the mirror. There was no visible sign of trauma unless he lifted his hair enough to see his scalp. The skin there was bruised and raw.

He popped a few painkillers and crashed into the recliner holding his cell phone. He tapped onto his contact list and held the phone to his ear.

"Hello?" Kate answered.

"Hey there. It's Barry. It happened again, Kate. When I went to sleep, I went back to that silent world."

There was a short pause on the other end.

"I'm at work right now, but I get off at seven. Any chance you'd like to meet up then? I want to hear what happened."

"Yeah. It was different this time. There are other people now... and creatures."

"Fuck. You sound shaken up, Barry. Are you all right?"

"Yeah. Just... I don't want to go back there again."

"Hey, don't sweat it. We'll come up with a plan. You won't go anywhere. I'll text you my address. Remember I'm in the garage, not the main house."

"Ok. Yeah. I'll see you around seven thirty then."

"And Barry?"

"Yeah, Kate?"

"Pick up a pizza, will ya? I do my best brainstorming when I'm full of pepperoni pizza."

Barry laughed. "Of course."

He hung up the call, leaned back in the chair with a huge grin on his face. Here he was, half a day away from being shot off into the void with killer phantoms and he was smiling over some girl.

He shook his head.

She seems pretty great though.

Barry stood outside Angelo's Pizza and Pasta patting his back pocket. There was no wallet. Barry had stupidly left it in his bathroom.

I just ruined the whole night.

Then memory struck. Barry crossed his fingers and went back to his truck. He plopped open the glove compartment. Sure enough, a thick stack of brand new hundred-dollar bills sat inside. He wiped the sweat from his brow and smiled.

Barry pulled up to the house at 7:30pm on the dot. His left knee was bouncing nervously, but he immediately felt some of the anxiety disappear the moment he spotted the Volkswagen in the driveway.

He parked behind the yellow vehicle and was approaching the garage door when it suddenly popped open. Kate's smiling face peered out at him.

"Hey, Barry. Come on in!"

Barry stepped inside and kicked off his shoes. He didn't know what to expect exactly, it being a garage apartment, but this wasn't it. The place looked incredible.

The whole living room had a remarkably trendy look to it. A huge TV sat dead center on the wall, and beside it hung some vintage movie posters. To the left of the room was a real neon sign, Barry could hear it hum. There were bookcases, in every available space, that were overflowing with novels. A small kitchenette was at the back of the room with a bathroom beside it. On the right was a staircase that led to a small second floor.

"Wow, this place looks great," said Barry. "I take it you're a reader?"

"Big time. Life's always more interesting in a book," she told him. "Go ahead and set the pizza on the counter. I already took out some paper plates and drinks."

Barry and Kate dished out a few slices and made their way to the couch. He took a seat at the end and couldn't help but notice Kate took the middle section to be closer to him.

"So, what happened this time? You said there were other people?" Kate asked.

"Two, yeah. Although, I only met one of them. A teenager named Owen. He saved my ass."

Barry blew on the hot slice of pizza and took a bite.

"Did he save you from the creatures you had mentioned?" she asked.

"Owen called them phantoms. I had gone back to the mall to watch another movie or two and this crazy black mist came in. It materialized into what Owen called a reaper. It legit looked just like the Grim Reaper. It even carried a scythe."

"What did you do?"

"Ran."

Kate laughed. "Then what?"

"Then a second one showed up, identical to the first. Just after that, Owen showed up on one of those electronic bikes. We took off across the city. We outran both phantoms. Owen spotted something, slammed on the brakes, and then I smashed my head off a car."

"What did he see?"

"No clue. When I woke up, I was in someone's basement. I think the kid dragged me into a house to keep me safe. His sweater was under my head when I woke up."

"You lost consciousness? Barry, that's not good. Did you go to a doctor?"

"No, I'm fine. I don't even have a headache anymore."

Kate put down the pizza crust and examined his head.

"So, you hit your head and remember a bunch of crazy stuff, huh?"

Barry laughed. "You got it! It's all real though, Kate. All of it."

"Ok, well I figured out a plan to keep you out of the phantom world," she said, looking quite serious.

Barry sat up and gave her his undivided attention.

"You're going to have to sleep here with me. That way I can keep an eye on you. I'll make sure you don't go anywhere."

Barry fought to suppress a smile. "Well, if you think that's best."

The hour grew late, and Kate led him up to her bedroom. They both stripped down to their underwear and slid under the covers.

Barry laid there nervously, unsure if he should make a move. It seemed like all the signs were there, but Barry had been mistaken before.

"Tell me why you'd ever want to step in front of a train," she whispered.

Barry took a deep breath. "I don't want to change the way you look at me."

"It won't, Barry. I promise."

After a long pause, Barry began.

"My little brother, Jay, and I, were all excited for Halloween. He was eleven. I was sixteen. He had talked me into trick-r-treating with him one last year. I was clearly too old to be doing it, but I could rarely say no to the kid. So, of course, we had matching costumes. I was a mustard bottle, and he was ketchup. Jay thought it was the funniest thing in the world."

A tear rolled down Barry's cheek. Kate reached forward and wiped it away with her thumb.

"School had let out early and my folks weren't home yet. We were trying to waste some time. Jay was shooting hoops in the driveway, while I sat on the porch playing on my cell phone.

"The ball must have hit his foot and shot out into the street. When I looked up, I saw him run into the road after it. The car struck him out of nowhere."

Barry's voice was hitching. He was struggling not to full blown cry in front of Kate.

"I ran to him... but he had died on impact. There were no final words between us. No goodbye."

"I'm so sorry, Barry," Kate said.

"My parents blamed me for it. They never came right out and said so, but they made it obvious enough. My dad left us. Moved across the country. He hasn't tried to contact me at all. My mother ignored me. Allowed her new husband to treat me like shit. I moved out and haven't spoken to mom since."

"Fuck, Barry. That's not your fault. None of it is your fault. It's just something horrible that happened. Your parents are assholes for not telling you that. They should have taken care of their son that was still here."

Kate leaned in and kissed him. Her lips were warm and soft against his own. He kissed her back.

"Hold me, Barry. And I'll hold you. I'll keep you right here with me. You won't go anywhere tonight."

That's how they fell asleep. Curled lovingly in each other's arms with eyes full of tears.

Barry woke to Kate's nose nuzzling his neck. He smiled.

"I told you it would work. I told I'd keep you here," she whispered.

Barry's eyes opened wide.

"You hear that?" he asked.

"No. I don't hear a thing."

"Exactly."

SEVEN

Kate jumped off the mattress and tugged open the bottom drawer of her dresser. There was some morning light filtering in through a small window above the bed, allowing Barry a much better view than the night before. She was bent at the waist pushing clothes around inside the drawer. Barry stared at the curves of her body. A pink lace thong trailed through two plump cheeks. He felt his pulse quicken. Only as she rose did Barry make out the faint lines across her wrists and forearms. Old scars.

Kate spun around holding a pair of black yoga pants. Her eyebrows wrinkled at the doofy look on Barry's face.

"Get your ass moving. I want to see this," she scolded.

She pushed her legs into the tight pants and threw on a pink long-sleeved shirt. She rushed down the stairs without another word.

Barry groaned and climbed out of bed. He bent over and scooped up his clothes from the carpeted floor.

As he made his way out to the driveway, he could see Kate at the road putting her golden hair up into a ponytail.

"It's so quiet! I didn't know it could be this quiet," she said. "Honestly Barry, it was fifty-fifty for me if you were a lunatic. Maybe closer to sixty-forty. But wow, you were for real, this is so wild! What are we going to do first? The whole world is ours!"

Barry loped over to the end of the driveway.

"You thought there was a good chance I was a nut job, and you still had me come over and spend the night? What the hell, Kate?"

"I thought I could help you work through some stuff. You seemed like a great guy other than one bizarre fantasy. You left out the part where you even *almost* got lucky too," she said elbowing him in the side.

Barry rubbed his temples in frustration.

"I don't know why you're so excited. There are phantoms remember. Phantoms that want to kill you, Kate. Please keep that in mind."

Kate turned her head from side to side. "I don't see any. Please, please, please can we go shopping? Everything is on a hundred percent discount right now."

Barry laughed. "I'm definitely not going back to that mall. And I believe that's technically stealing your talking about."

"Eh, some big box chain isn't going to miss it. Come on."

"Well, I can't really pass judgement with ten grand sitting in my glove compartment."

Kate playfully slapped his shoulder. "Barry!"

He laughed again.

"First things first though. I need to head into Arlington and get to the clock tower. We can meet up with the boys and see if they have any answers to what's going on. We need to know what this place is."

"Let's roll!" Kate said, heading for Barry's truck.

"Hold up. Do you mind if we take your bug? It's a lot quieter and I don't want to make us a target out there with my loud exhaust."

"Sure, but you're driving. I'll be the DJ!"

They circled around to the yellow Volkswagen and Barry started to climb inside. Kate just stood there by the door; her head cocked to one side.

"What?" asked Barry.

"I thought you said there were no animals here, Barry," she said stepping away from the vehicle and circling around back of the garage. Barry pulled himself out of the car and followed.

As he was coming around the garage, he heard it too. A loud meow coming from just inside the wood line. As Kate crossed the lawn, Barry got an uneasy feeling in the pit of his stomach.

"Kate, don't," he said in a harsh whisper.

She turned to look at him. Behind her a lumbering red-skinned creature burst from the trees. It was humanoid but its face was contorted. Its body was covered in shiny scales. Tendrils of red smoke drifted off its body as it rushed at the pair.

Kate ran for her life.

"Get to the car," Barry shouted as he broke into his own run.

Barry thought a creature that size should make a noise while it ran. Its feet slapping hard against the ground or deep puffs of air from its nostrils as it moved. Yet, Barry heard nothing but silence behind them.

As he reached the end of the lawn, he chanced a look behind him. It wasn't as slow as the reaper, this one was as fast as they were. The phantom had closed the considerable distance between them, almost on top of Kate as she pumped her arms furiously.

With how silently these things moved, if Barry wasn't constantly checking his surroundings in this world, he'd be dead before he knew what happened.

Sitting on a park bench, enjoying an afternoon, he'd never hear one of these things come up behind him. He imagined feeling those scaley hands close around his throat.

The pair ran around the side of the garage. Barry reached the car first, threw himself inside and started the engine. He slammed it into reverse and waited as Kate circled the vehicle. She ripped open the door. The creature reached the front of the car and was bringing down its gigantic fist as Barry floored it. Kate was barely inside as the little car skidded into the road. Barry sent it sailing down the quiet street.

A few minutes had passed, and the pair were able to catch their breath. Barry blew out a long stream of air.

"So that was pretty wild, huh?" she asked.

"Yeah, that's why we should always be on guard. And not go off looking for kittens."

"It sounded so real. Lured me right in," she said laughing.

She turned up the music and began to move to the rhythm, like she hadn't almost died three minutes prior. Barry immediately grew concerned Kate wasn't taking this whole thing seriously enough.

"Stop off at the party supply store before we get to the clocktower please," said Kate.

Barry pulled onto the highway.

"Why?"

"They sell costumes. I'd like to meet these fellas dressed like a clown. Full makeup, the works."

"Yeah, we're not doing that."

"Don't be a party pooper, Barry. From what that kid told you, this Johnny guy will be all brooding and serious. I'll waddle up to him in my huge clown shoes and when he says I need to take this more seriously, I'll honk my big red clown nose."

Barry laughed so hard that he had tears form at the corner of his eyes.

"You like to make really weird first impressions, don't you?"

"It's my trademark."

The clock tower was easy enough to find. It loomed in the center of the city and was leagues taller than all the buildings that surrounded it. It was made of light gray brick and had a huge clockface on each of its four sides.

Barry pulled up outside the building and opened the car door. The wind had picked up and the few small trees that lined the street were rustling, making noise in the usually silent world.

Kate, absent of a clown suit, followed him to the front door and pulled the huge brass handle. The door opened with ease.

They walked across the waxed lobby floor and pressed the call button for the aging elevator. There was a loud ding as the doors separated.

"So, Barry, would you rather only eat pickles the rest of your life, no other food, or attend a Nickelback concert every single month until the day you die?"

Barry climbed into the elevator and pressed the button for the top floor. If the guys weren't in the lobby, maybe they were up on the observation deck.

"You don't get sick from the pickles, it's enough nutrition, and at the concert you can't be on your phone or distracted by anything, you have to pay attention."

The doors closed and they began to rise.

Barry thought for a moment. "The concert for sure. I get to travel the country and see a kickass rock band. There's no downside."

Kate wore a look of disgust. "Ew, Barry."

The elevator dinged and the doors rolled open. Standing in the middle of the room was Owen with a look of surprise on his face. Behind him, on the outdoor deck, was an older man wearing a jean jacket. He was surveying the city with binoculars.

"Barry," Owen shouted, "I was worried you were dead, man."

At the sound of Owen's raised voice, Johnny turned away from the view and made his way inside.

"Crap! I forgot your hoodie. It's in my truck," said Barry. "Did you drag me all the way down to that basement by yourself?"

"I sure did. You're one heavy bastard too," said Owen. "I went back to the house in the regular world and tried to find you. I got too late of a start though, my parents had like five hundred chores for me, and when I finally got there, you were gone. I tried your apartment after that. You live above a barbershop, right? You weren't there either. I was nervous something had happened to you."

"Whoa... whoa... slow down. You cross over from the real world like me?"

A grisly voice spoke up from the back of the room. "There are two main types of people that find their way here. Sleepers, like you and Owen, and then my kind."

The old man crossed the room and took a seat in a metal folding chair.

"You must be Johnny. I'm Barry, and this is Kate."

"Pleased to meet you," said Kate.

"Yeah, the boy told me about you already. I'm surprised you're still alive. I don't know the girl's story though," said Johnny.

"She crossed over with me this morning," said Barry.

"That's mighty peculiar," said the old man.

"So, you were saying there were two types of people that make it here? What type does that make you? And where is *here* exactly?"

"Oh, I can tell you where we are," said Owen.

"Hush up, boy. You've done enough with that story of yours. Two dead. Those souls are on you," Johnny said gruffly. "Truth is, no one knows what this place is. I suspect it's Hell though. I'm not inclined to know why you sleepers come here, but I know why I did. I died and I didn't live a godly life. This is where my soul went."

Barry and Kate's eyes met.

"There are some things you'll want to know, if you plan on staying alive," said Johnny. "The first is to move around. Don't go to the same building two days in a row. Something happens, like our scent collects in a place, and it draws them there. Same thing happens when a few of us are together, they pick up on the scent quicker. That's why we can't linger here for more than a few hours. There's never been four of us together like this but there's been three of us several times. They come on quick. I imagine with the four of us, the phantoms will be swarming this building before early evening. That's why you were almost killed at the mall. Your scent had collected there already, you went back and added more."

Barry turned to Owen. "Yeah, so again, a big thank you for saving my ass. But tell me, what the hell did you see to make you slam on those brakes?"

"Sorry about that. Your head left a killer dent in that car," said Owen. "Anyway, I saw one of the night searchers. It was in the middle of the street in broad daylight. I'd never seen one out during the day before."

"Another peculiar thing," Johnny said, scratching his face.

"What's a searcher?" asked Kate.

"A type of phantom. They all wear dark green robes, but they aren't identical. They all have different faces. Faces of men. They carry a lantern and search for people at night."

"What happens if they find you?" Kate asked.

"No idea. I'm not trying to find out either."

"Maybe they just want to tuck you in and give you a little kiss goodnight," said Kate.

Barry and Owen both laughed.

"I don't think you're taking this seriously enough," said Johnny.

Kate smacked Barry's arm. "I told you he would say that! And now I don't have a clown nose to honk."

Johnny gave the couple a measuring look. "The phantoms are also attracted to noise. So, try to be as quiet as possible. Especially while traveling. Also, you may have discovered you can affect things in the real world while you're here. We don't know how it works exactly, but it seems you can only change things if it doesn't give away this place."

"How do you mean?" asked Barry.

"Send an email, leave a voicemail, leave a note on a table telling people about the phantom realm and none of them will be there the next day. Move a chair from one side of the room to another and that change will stick. I once burned down an entire building to see if it would transfer to the other side. Sometime in the early hours of the morning, the building reverted right back to normal. Not an ounce of damage."

"How long have you guys been here?" Kate asked.

"Owen has been here twenty-two days now, forty-four if you count both sides. I've lost count on my time here. Somewhere in the ballpark of seven months."

"Oh my God, you've been trapped here for seven months?" said Kate.

"And stayed alive. That's why you need to listen to me. My last piece of advice is to ignore what Owen will surely tell you and just run. You see a phantom, you run.

You hide when you're far enough away. Something Barry learned on his second day here, but it's good advice all the same," said Johnny. "So, tell me, Barry. Did you not see a phantom your entire first day? Why the hell would you go back to that mall?"

"No, I never saw anything my first day."

"No strange noises? No unexplained cold drafts?"

"Nothing other than the chain sticks out in my mind."

Johnny and Owen gave each other a quick look.

"What do you mean chain?" Johnny asked.

"It was nothing really. I just heard a metal chain dragging through the mall. I couldn't find anyone though. I assumed it was one of the pull chains on the overhead doors rattling."

Johnny grew even more serious.

"Owen and I had this idea to travel underground using the sewer system. I figured if we could learn to navigate the tunnels, we could sneak around the city without being spotted. But when we got down there, we were in for a surprise. There are creatures everywhere down there. All over the tunnels. They're no threat up here because they're all chained in place. The chain is long enough for them to move from wall to wall. Just enough room to grab someone who tries to pass by. These creatures are... awful. If any of them got loose...

if they made it above ground... I'd have to leave the city."

Suddenly all four of them jerked their heads toward the stairs. A floating white phantom hovered there with his head lolled back. It was letting out an ear-piercing shriek. Barry's eardrums vibrated in his skull. Kate pressed her palms against her ears.

Johnny shouted to them. They could barely hear him over the phantom. "It'll bring dozens of others! Everybody, run!"

EIGHT

"You three take the stairs all the way down to level eight. On the east side of the building there is a fire escape. Take it down to the street and for God's sake, don't let any of those things see you," yelled Johnny.

"How does he know that?" asked Kate, moving toward the stairwell.

"We always scout the buildings. Gotta have an exit strategy," Owen shouted over the phantom.

Johnny moved to the ghostly white shrieker and kicked his boot toward it.

"Attention on me, asshole," Johnny yelled at the ghastly creature.

The phantom paid no mind. It drifted behind Owen as he stepped onto the staircase.

Kate and Barry barreled down the steps as fast as their legs would take them. The shrieks echoed down the entire stairwell. The sound was maddening.

Owen turned to Johnny. "I can shake it. No worries."

"No kid, your death isn't gonna be on my hands," Johnny said swinging his arm in front of the spectral body.

The phantom's attention never waned. It continued in pursuit of the teenage boy. Its head was tilted back, screeching that high pitched noise, but its eyes never moved. It remained fixed on the ceiling as it drifted behind Owen.

"Don't think we have a choice, buddy." said Owen. "I can handle it. You just do your thing at the rooftop."

Johnny scowled and nodded. He made his way back to the outer deck and started yelling. Maybe he could buy the lad some time and steer the incoming crowd toward himself.

Barry reached the eighth floor completely out of breath and threw open the window labeled "Emergency Exit." He climbed onto the rusted platform; heavy wind pushed at his back. Below him the street was filled with patches of different colored clouds of smoke.

"What the hell? There isn't a couple of dozen. There's nearly a hundred," said Kate, following Barry's gaze.

Owen reached the open window. "I'll wait here until you guys hit the ground. Stay behind anything you can; cars, trash cans, whatever. The less chance of them sensing you, the better."

Barry was staring down at the street. "We're going to die."

"Probably! Now move it! This shrieker is bringing all those things right to me. Some are probably inside the building already," Owen yelled.

Barry wasted no time. He dropped to his knees and swung his feet onto the corroded metal ladder. It felt less than stable, but Barry had no time to dwell on it. He raced down to the next platform and repeated the action. Overhead, Kate struggled to keep up.

Barry made it to the last platform, just feet above the street. Below him a mist of dark blue floated up to a glass window. He watched as it seeped in through the cracks that surrounded the frame. They were getting inside the building.

Barry studied the landscape in front of him. The street was filled with thick black clouds speckled with reds, greens, pinks, different shades of blues, and yellows. Barry wondered what horrors each of them would manifest into but made no plan to hang around and find out. Kate finally dropped onto the platform beside him, panting.

"There's some decent breaks between them coming up there and there," Barry said, pointing. "If we can slide under that big truck we can make it to that hotel, no problem. Then we can wait it out in there."

Kate had nothing smart to say, no joke to crack. She just nodded her head. Beads of sweat rolled down her face despite the wind and cool air.

Barry grabbed her under the arms and lowered her to the ground just behind some disappearing red fog. Kate squatted low to the ground and rushed to hide behind a large post office box. She waited for another opening.

Overhead, Barry heard the sound of shattering glass amongst the everlasting shrieking. He looked up in time to see Owen drop from the top platform to the next, never touching the ladder. Bits of rusted metal and shards of glass rained down on Barry's upturned face. A sledgehammer was pulled through the window back inside the building. Barry couldn't see what was wielding it.

Owen dropped down to the fourth level platform with the shrieker floating down behind him. The kid was fast, moved like a damn ninja.

Barry felt the urgency and scurried down to the street.

Through clenched teeth he told Kate, "We have to move. Now."

Kate saw a space between a yellow and a black blob of mist floating toward the building and ran between the two. She dropped flat to the ground and rolled under the lifted truck.

Barry watched in horror as the black smoke solidified into a reaper. It lowered its cloaked head to peer at Kate under the vehicle.

"Oh, fuck!" she yelled and rolled to the other side of the truck.

The reaper floated soundlessly around the vehicle. The scythe gleamed in the daylight as it swayed in the creature's boney hands.

Kate broke into an all-out run, right past the hotel doors and inside the neighboring building. Barry couldn't tell what the building was from his angle, but he did see the reaper follow her inside.

The shrieks grew louder behind Barry, and he turned to see Owen drop into the street.

"Now would be a good time to run," Owen shouted.

All around them, the phantoms began to materialize. Barry lowered his head and charged across the street. His plan was to follow Kate inside her building, but the way was blocked. Barry had to break left and enter the hotel as previously planned.

Outside, Owen ran by phantoms of various shapes and sizes. Many of which Owen had never seen before. The shrieker remained fixed to his heels as he pushed himself to move faster. Owen had a plan. Maybe not a great one. But escape was just two blocks away.

Barry climbed inside the elevator and pressed the button labeled "Penthouse." The slow ascent felt like it took forever but in reality, it was less than a minute.

He rushed to the end of the hallway to a large window, trying to catch a glimpse of the teenager and those who chased him. Instead, he saw Johnny rush past the window. He was steering a long, red, rectangular parachute with hand-held grips. He soared down the street like a bird and rounded a corner sharply, disappearing from view.

"How the hell..." Barry mumbled.

Below him, Owen had made great headway with an army of creatures parading after him. The shrieker never far behind.

The teen pumped his arms as he forced himself to keep an unnatural pace. He was there, on the bridge, just needed to get a little more center.

Something howled behind him. Owen refused to turn and look at whatever made the sound. His imagination went wild with possibilities. Could it be a werewolf? Some huge, hairy beast that was half man and half wolf closing in behind him? Owen pictured its jaws snapping down on the back of his neck. Tears started to form in his eyes as he felt a wave of panic washing over him. This was it, now or never.

Owen reached the railing, grabbed hold, and swung his feet over in one fluid motion. He dropped over the edge and continued to fall five stories into a rushing river. He smacked against the water hard, driving the air from his lungs as he dipped below the cold surface.

Barry hadn't witnessed any of that, just saw the extensive line of phantoms being led away from the clock tower.

He walked down the hall to one of the suites and tried the door. It opened without a key or keycard. Nothing in this world seemed to be very secure.

Barry stepped inside. It was set up like a full apartment. He crossed the living room with a light blue couch facing a large television mounted to the wall. He reached a window that faced the neighboring building.

His eyes darted from window to window, searching for some sign of Kate. She had the very same idea and two levels below, Barry spotted her. Their eyes met and Kate smiled. She lifted her hand in a subtle wave and gave him a thumbs up. It looked like she was all right.

Barry blew out a long sigh of relief. Strangely, he could see his breath.

Huh?

He blew again and watched the puff of white mist float from his mouth. Only then did Barry realize how cold it was inside the suite.

The room was suddenly filled with a child's giggle. The sound seemed to be everywhere at once, reverberating off each wall. There was no way to tell where the laughter was coming from.

Barry slowly scanned the suite. In the bedroom doorframe stood a little girl with jet black hair draped over her face. She wore a white dress full of ruffles. Her skin was a sickly gray.

The giggling turned into screams as Barry backed into the wall. Only it wasn't the phantom that produced the screams. It was Barry. He had finally snapped.

NINE

Kate had just stepped away from the window when she heard the muffled scream from the building next door. She threw open the window and contorted herself for a better view. The window Barry had been seen in just a moment before was frosted over. The neighboring windows were also covered in ice.

"Shit!" she yelled.

She knew the reaper that had followed her into the building was still in there someplace. She just didn't know where. There was no time to stress over it. She had to risk it and get to Barry.

Kate yanked open the door and peered down both sides of the hall. It was clear. She made a mad dash to the corner stairwell and started taking the steps down two at a time.

Barry stood there, frozen, staring at the little girl with gray skin. His back was against the wall, unable to retreat any further.

The girl titled her head back and laughed again. The giggle echoed through the suite. It sounded to Barry like it was coming out of every wall. He felt surrounded, suffocated.

The girl reached both of her arms across her belly and drew a knife from each side. She wore an old-timey dress with no pockets; it made no sense to Barry where the girl would have concealed the blades.

The thought was short lived as she dashed forward.

Only at the last second did Barry snap out of it and sidestep the rushing phantom.

He felt the creature's damp hair slap against his left arm and a burning sensation across his chest.

He looked down to see that the entity had caught him with one of the blades. His shirt was slashed over his pectoral muscle. Blood began running down his abdomen.

Barry rushed for the front door to the suite and tore it open. He was producing a completely involuntary sound that wasn't quite a scream, not quite a growl, it was something in between the two.

He didn't chance a look behind him at first. The phantoms moved in silence, and he was sure it was almost upon him.

Barry ran full speed down the hallway until his shoulder collided with the stairwell door. It bashed against a radiator with a loud crack. He made it down two flights of stairs before he finally dared to glance behind him. A gray cloud of smoke fluttered down the staircase at a slow but steady pace. He didn't have much of a lead.

Barry hurried on, stopping just before he reached the bottom floor when he heard the door below clang shut.

He waited and listened for another sound.

"Barry?" a tentative voice called.

He rushed to the bottom and grabbed Kate by the arm.

"How many are outside?"

"The entire side street is empty at the moment," she answered.

Barry pushed out of the exit and ran hand in hand with Kate for three blocks before he felt it was safe enough to stop. They took a moment to catch their breath.

"My God, Barry! You're bleeding!" Kate practically yelled.

"Quiet. Don't alert those things," he ordered. "The phantom cut me. I'll be fine. I don't think it's deep."

"Which phantom?"

"I haven't seen this one before. Have you seen that horror movie where the dead girl is in the attic and lurches out at the guy that sticks his head up there?"

"I think it's a woman that puts her head up there."

"Regardless, it resembled her but with knives."

"Yeah, no thanks."

She pulled his shirt off over his head and dabbed the wound carefully with the cloth.

"You got lucky. It's not too bad," she told him.

She pressed the balled-up shirt hard against the wound to stifle the last bit of bleeding.

"Hold it there," she said, surveying their surroundings.

"I think there's a department store a few blocks that way. We should be far enough from the clock tower to relax. We can find you a new shirt."

"I knew you'd find a way to turn this into a shopping trip," he said with a grin.

Kate slapped his shoulder playfully and tugged him in the direction of the store.

Overhead, dark gray clouds rolled in. The wind had already been bad, but it increased tenfold. Gusts pushed them sideways as they continued along the road.

Right as the store came into view the skies opened up and began dumping heavy rain. By the time they reached the actual storefront, the pair were soaked from head to toe.

The door pulled open easily and they stepped inside. Kate lifted the shirt away from the cut on Barry's chest. The bleeding had stopped. Her hand lingered on his chest as she looked up into his eyes. He slowly lowered his face and pressed his lips softly against hers.

Barry pulled away but kept his eyes on hers. A smile spread across Kate's face. He grabbed her by the waist and pulled her in more roughly this time. He kissed her forcefully. An obvious desire had taken hold of him.

This time Kate was the one to pull away.

"Settle down, lover boy. Go find some dry clothes. I'll run to the ladies' section and meet you at the dressing room."

Barry chuckled to himself as he moved to the racks of clothes. After several minutes perusing, he had selected a maroon polo shirt, a pair of black Chinos, as well as dry socks and underwear.

He glanced around the department store until he spotted a sign labelled "fitting rooms." Barry made his way over and stripped off his wet clothing. He tore open the package of boxer briefs and put a pair on. Then he did the same with a pair of black ankle socks.

There was a light knock on the changing room door.

Barry swung open the door and was awestruck by the sight. Kate was in the sexiest lingerie he'd ever laid eyes on. It was some sort of lace corset with bits of red satin covering her breasts and sides. Below that she wore a black pleated satin skirt that left little to the imagination.

Kate threw her cell phone next to Barry's on the bench.

Barry didn't remember standing up or crossing the room. He was just suddenly holding Kate against the wall. Her squeals of excitement in his ear quickly turned into moans of pleasure as they writhed together.

The two of them crumpled to the floor when they were finished. Kate was panting. Her barely covered breasts heaving up and down with deep breaths. Barry watched her with a satisfied grin.

"Impressive performance Mr. Abrams," said Kate, meeting his eyes.

They were both laughing when the sledgehammer smashed through the drywall between them.

Kate screamed. Barry jumped to his feet and pulled Kate up by the arm. He pushed her out of the dressing room and scooped up his clothes. A colossal arm reached through the drywall trying to snatch him.

"Run!" he yelled.

Kate charged toward the front door with Barry just feet behind her. A lumbering muscular creature wearing an ornate metal helmet tore itself free from the wall. Dust and plaster puffed from the falling wreckage at the phantom's feet.

"Go! Don't stop!" Barry yelled.

Kate shot into the street. The lingerie she wore was immediately soaked through in the torrential downpour.

Barry wrapped his arm around her waist and tugged her along. They ran for two blocks, checking behind them as they went. The rain was falling so hard it was impossible to tell if they were being followed.

"There!" Barry called to Kate.

He was pointing to a large U-Haul parked on the side of the street.

Kate ran to the back and lifted the thick metal latch. Barry lifted the overhead door and helped Kate inside. He rolled in behind her and slammed the door closed.

"Now what?" Kate asked, panting in the darkness.

Barry unfurled the wad of clothing and pulled out their cellphones. He turned on the flashlight app and scanned the back of the truck. There were several carboard boxes, a plastic-wrapped dresser, and a large three-piece couch.

"I guess we wait out the storm and pray nothing finds us back here," he said.

"Come keep me warm," she said climbing onto the couch.

Barry followed her over and curled up against her body. He draped his damp polo over her legs and put his arm around her. He softly stroked the silky fabric on her side and listened to the rain patter against the metal roof. It wasn't long before the pair drifted off to sleep.

TEN

Barry woke to the sound of the U-Haul's overhead door sliding open on its tracks. He sat up quickly and watched a middle-aged man with graying hair drop a large cardboard box to the ground.

"What the hell?" the man shouted.

Barry shook Kate awake and tugged on the pair of chinos that were lying on the couch next to him. Kate slowly rose and surveyed the scene. The man's eyes lingered on Kate, still in her lingerie.

"What? Were you guys back here fucking?" the man said with more humor in his voice than anger.

Barry pulled the polo shirt off the cushion and slid it over Kate's head. It mostly covered her. Only a little of her butt poked out from the bottom.

"No, sir. We were just trying to get out of the rain and must have dozed off. We'll get out of here," Barry explained.

"It hasn't rained in a damn week," said the man, stepping to the side.

Barry jumped to the road in his sock feet and took Kate by the hand. She jumped from the rig and the two of them began running down the sidewalk.

"Couple of God damn nutjobs," the guy yelled behind them.

Kate laughed. Her bare feet slapped loudly against the sidewalk as they slowed their pace.

"This is a real walk of shame, Barry. The clock tower is like five blocks away," Kate said between deep breaths.

They were turning heads as they went along. It couldn't have been more than fifty degrees, and Barry was shirtless. Kate looked naked from the waist down.

As they reached their destination and rounded the huge clock tower onto Main Street, they both stopped in their tracks. Owen was leaning against the yellow Volkswagen with a grin on his face. He too was barefoot.

"I can only imagine what you guys have been up to," he teased.

"Owen!" Kate shouted and rushed at the boy.

Although she barely knew him, she threw her arms around him. Owen's face immediately flushed red with a blush. Barry slapped a meaty hand on his shoulder and squeezed.

"Glad to see you're all right. How the hell did you get away from all those phantoms?" Barry asked.

"Most of them are mega-slow, easy to outpace. That shrieker was tricky though. I had to jump into the river to lose it. Almost drowned too. Piece of advice, don't jump into a river with your shoes on."

"Damn smart thinking," said Barry.

Kate moved around to the driver's side door and unlocked the car.

"Can we give you a lift?" she asked.

"Yeah," he answered. "Say, you guys have any plans today?"

Kate and Barry looked at each other.

"I don't think so. Why?" Kate asked.

"Well, if you're up to it, I can explain what causes the phantom rift and what the phantom realm really is. I can also take you somewhere to help prove it."

A smile spread across Barry's face.

"Hell yeah. Let's go."

The first order of business was to get everyone back to their homes to get proper clothing. Kate was driving, so naturally she drove to her place first.

The morning was quickly warming up, and Kate exited her apartment with a twirl causing her skirt to flutter in the air. She wore a maroon-colored long-sleeved shirt for a top. Barry assumed this was the norm for her, sweaters and long-sleeved shirts to hide her scars.

She approached the car with a huge smile on her face. Barry thought she was in a surprisingly good mood for someone that just left a shadow realm full of killer phantoms. Especially since they'd be back there trying to survive in less than twenty-four hours.

That was the weird thing about Kate. She didn't have appropriate responses to a lot of situations. For example, that mimic phantom, the one meowing just inside the woods. It had almost caught and did God know what to them, yet two minutes after a near death experience she's back to goofing around like nothing ever happened.

Barry assumed it had to do with whatever her therapist was treating her for. Tonight, he'd strike up a conversation about the scars and the carefree attitude. He wouldn't do it now in front of the boy. Their relationship had gotten physical and if they were to become a real couple, it would all need to come to light.

Kate climbed into the driver's seat.

"Oh, shit. Hold up," said Barry, climbing out of the Volkswagen.

He jogged over to his truck, still in Kate's driveway, and pulled open the squealing door.

He ran back over and tossed something at Owen in the back seat as he plopped down.

"Yes! My hoodie! Thanks, man. I was worried I wouldn't see it again," said Owen.

"Made for a great pillow. Might want to run it through the wash, may have gotten some blood on it from the ol' noggin," Barry said with a laugh.

Kate backed out of the driveway and Owen gave directions to his parents' house. Turned out he lived right in Orchard Bay, just two blocks from Barry's apartment. What a small world.

He ran into the house and scooped up a pair of shoes before his parents could notice him. He didn't need the third degree over where he'd been all morning.

Barry ran into his apartment next. He changed into an old pair of jeans and a tight-fitting black tee.

"Ok, so where are we off to, Owen?" Kate asked as Barry reentered the car.

"Main highway, like we're going right back to Arlington."

Owen gave step by step directions off the ramp, through a little suburb north of the city. Eventually he pointed to a small parking lot beside a two-story brick building. Kate drove into the closest parking spot.

Barry turned in his seat and said, "All right. We're here. We're ready to know the whole deal."

Owen took a deep breath and leaned forward in his seat.

"So, tell me, have you two spent any time in a psychiatric center? Or do you just see a therapist? Or do I have it wrong and you just suffer from undiagnosed depression?"

Kate actually looked startled for once. Barry let out a single laugh.

"Why would you ask that?" asked Barry.

"Because that's the key to the phantom rift. I'm right, aren't I? You two have some kind of psych history."

"We met at our therapist's shared office," said Barry. "I don't understand what that has to do with anything though."

"The phantom realm boils down to one thing. It's a place the mentally ill go to either get better, to reignite their will to live... or to die."

"I'm not sure I'm following," said Kate.

"Have you ever heard someone use the phrase 'they lost the battle with their demons' before? Whether they're aware of it or not, they're speaking literally. Somehow, we instinctively know about the phantom realm or enough people have gone there to spread the knowledge," Owen explained. "Just think about the reaper. It's the most common phantom. The Grim Reaper is a well-known pop culture entity. Where did that start? I bet it's from people going to the phantom realm throughout history."

"Why wouldn't it be like common knowledge though? If so many people go there, wouldn't we have already heard of the place?" asked Kate.

"Not when the people that go there have a psych history. Who's going to believe them? People are just going to think they're crazy," said Owen. "I haven't shared my experience with any of my friends or family. Too afraid I'll end up locked in a padded cell."

"So, you think this is like a mental gymnasium? You work through your problems, find that will to live and then what? The rift between the worlds just closes up?" Barry asked with his eyebrows raised.

"Well, yeah. But it's more than that. I think we have to work up the nerve to battle our demons. We fight the phantoms," said Owen with a measuring look.

"This is why Johnny warned us not to listen to you, isn't it? He said you got two people killed with this theory," said Kate.

"He says I got them killed, but we don't really know if it worked or not. I appreciate everything Johnny has done for me, but he's not always right about this stuff," said Owen.

"What's he wrong about, Owen?" Barry asked.

"I'm glad you asked. This brings me to the show and tell portion of our trip," Owen said with a grin.

The three of them exited the vehicle and made their way to the front entrance. The sign above the door read "Happy Valley Long Term Care Facility." They weaved down two hallways. A nurse seemed to recognize Owen and waved. They stopped outside room 1134.

"Johnny likes to tell people that two types of people come to the phantom realm. Sleepers and the dead. That's what he's wrong about," Owen said pushing open the door.

There on the hospital bed was a man hooked up to all kinds of tubes and pumps keeping him breathing. He was ghostly pale, but they knew immediately who they were looking at. Johnny.

"There's only one type of person that travels through the rift... sleepers."

ELEVEN

Kate moved to the bedside and took Johnny's hand in hers.

"What happened to him?" she asked.

"Attempted suicide," Owen answered. "Only Johnny thinks he was successful, instead of lying here in a coma."

"Wait, so he doesn't know he's still alive?" Barry asked.

"I've tried to tell him. Whenever I bring it up, he starts yelling, won't let me explain. He just loses it, Barry. It's the same way he acts whenever I ask him what's down in the sewer."

"Huh? I thought you knew what was down there. Didn't he say you went into the sewer with him?"

"I did go down. Only, he made me wait by the ladder until he knew it was safe. He came running back after a few minutes and I never saw the creatures myself.

Whatever he saw down there put the fear of God into him. You should have seen his face."

"All right, so tomorrow we will meet up with Johnny and we will make him listen to us. Simple as that. We explain that he's still alive and convince him to come back with us. Then the four of us pin down and kill a phantom," said Kate.

"A few problems there. The first being, I have no clue where Johnny will be. We never discussed it before all hell broke loose. So, that means we'll have to find him before we can do anything. Secondly, convincing him is much easier said than done. Johnny is one stubborn son of a bitch, pardon my French. Lastly, I don't think we can all gang up on one phantom. We each need to take on our own," Owen explained.

They sat in silence for a moment. The group was lost in thought.

"Okay, so, we'll drop you off at home now. We'll come back and pick you up first thing in the morning after we slip back into the phantom realm. After that, we head to Arlington and start our search for Johnny. We'll pray things go our way and we can kill at least one of those things before nightfall. Best case scenario is that we destroy all four of our phantoms and celebrate like hell tomorrow. You guys in?"

"I am," said Kate.

"Absolutely," said Owen.

Kate dropped Owen off at his family's large blue townhouse. She turned to Barry in her seat.

"Am I dropping you off at your apartment, or do you want to grab your truck at my place?"

Barry face twisted a little in surprise. He grew quiet as he searched his mind for the right words.

"We... we aren't sticking together?"

Kate grabbed Barry's bicep with both hands and squeezed.

"It's Sunday, Barry. I have to work. We don't all have banker hours, ya know?"

Barry's face lightened.

"I can come over after if you want. I'll bring dinner! How's that sound?" Kate asked.

"That sounds great. I guess I'll take a ride back to your place and grab my truck, if you're heading that way anyway."

Barry drove his clunker back to the apartment. He found a parking spot right in front of the barber shop.

Barry went upstairs and plopped into his recliner. Only he didn't pick up the remote and surf channels like usual. Instead, he pondered Owen's theory and thought about how he would actually fight a phantom. Fight a phantom and win, preferably.

When the sun lowered in the sky, Barry showered and paced around his place until there was a loud knock on his door. He walked over and twisted the handle.

"Hope you like Chinese. I got us quite the variety," said Kate.

"I love it," said Barry. "How was work?"

"An absolute snoozefest in comparison to the phantom realm. Are we even sure you'll pull me back in with you again?"

Barry took out two plates and a couple of forks. He set them on the oak table in front of them.

"I think you're in the thick of it no matter what now, honestly. But if Owen's theory is correct, it was probably the depressing story of my brother that was the trigger to pull you in. Maybe tonight you could tell me about your scars. Kind of recreate the same conditions before we go to sleep."

A look of panic flashed over Kate's face. She almost dropped a carton of beef and broccoli onto the floor.

"Yeah, I suppose we could do that," she squeaked.

It was eleven o'clock in the evening. The lights in Barry's bedroom were off. Moonlight drifted through the closed window. He could barely see Kate's face just inches from his own.

"You sleepy?" he asked.

"Yeah," she whispered back.

"Now might be the time to start. What's your story, Kate?"

She let out a long sigh.

"It started at my school's talent show. I was in tenth grade and was not exceedingly popular. For some reason I had it in my mind that I was a great singer. I went out on stage with this crazy fantasy that I would blow away everyone with my amazing voice and instantly become one of the popular girls. Barry, I was terrible. The whole crowd was laughing at me. I even saw teachers fighting to hold back their smirks.

"I was so embarrassed. I felt so stupid for being so confident. I ran home and I felt like I had to do something with all those bottled-up feelings. I wasn't trying to end my life. I just needed a release. That was the first time I cut myself.

"After that, I started cutting more and more to deal with my feelings. I failed a test; I'd cut. Someone made fun of my shoes; I'd cut. It went on like that for almost a year. It was impossible to hide it from my parents forever. They eventually saw the damage I had caused.

"They admitted me to a psychiatric hospital for a bit. Eventually I traded cutting for dry humor. Better of course but I was still avoiding dealing with my feelings. That's what Dr. Williams and I are working on now. Appropriate responses to stress."

Even in the dark room, Barry could see her cheeks were streaked with tears. He put his arm around her.

"I'm so sorry, Kate."

"You know what's funny though, Barry? I had some normal reactions in the phantom realm. Between the clock tower and traveling back through the rift. I didn't have time for any of my bullshit. I didn't really deflect at all. I was dealing with all my crap in the present."

As that last sentence hung in the air, Barry leaned in and kissed her. They laid their heads back against the soft pillows, drifted to sleep, and passed through to the other side.

Barry opened his eyes and saw Kate still curled up beside him. An extreme silence filled the small apartment and the world outside.

"Rise and shine, sweetheart. We've got phantom ass to kick," Barry told her.

Her eyes still closed, she shifted in her twisted cocoon of blankets.

"Coffee," she muttered.

Barry laughed.

"I'll get a pot brewing. TO GO."

Barry exited the bedroom and jumped at the sound of a loud knock at the front door. Barry cautiously raised his eye to the peephole and then swung the door open wide.

"You guys sleeping in this morning?" said Owen, stepping inside the apartment.

"Kate is," Barry answered. "I'm fixing her some coffee and then we can head out."

"Hey, kid," Kate said, passing the two of them.

She was on her way to the bathroom, wearing incredibly skimpy shorts and a tank top. Owen's face grew red as an apple.

"Hey," Owen responded as cooly as he could muster.

The three of them took their travel mugs full of boiling hot Folgers and made their way to the street. Barry noticed a black electric bike leaning against his truck.

"Hop in, boys," said Kate, climbing into the yellow bug. "Where we off to exactly?"

"Johnny will be high up somewhere for surveillance. We haven't been to Palace Plaza in a while. There's a good chance he'll go there," said Owen. "And if not, it has a fantastic view of the city. We might be able to spot him on another building."

"Let's roll," said Kate, pressing too hard on the gas pedal.

Both Barry and Owen's head slammed into their headrests. Owen chuckled.

As they made their way to the plaza, Owen kept an eye out for phantoms. The only one he spotted was in at the bookshop on 2nd Street. Something with long spidery legs was scurrying up the side of the brick building. He said a quick prayer that it wouldn't spot the vehicle rushing by.

When they pulled up to the front of the plaza a few minutes later, Owen said, "The three of us should be all right searching the building but if we find Johnny, at least one of us will need to break away from the group. You guys saw how fast things got out of control at the clock tower when all four of us were together."

"That was mostly the shrieker's fault though, right" Kate asked.

"Yeah, but the four of us drew a shrieker in fast."

Barry nodded in agreement and led the way inside.

There were no signs of Johnny or any phantoms in the main lobby. Everything looked so clean; fresh wax on the floor, counters polished. Barry tapped the button to call the elevator, and the doors opened at once. They piled inside.

"What gives? It says it only goes to level fifteen. This is one of the tallest buildings in the city, it has to go higher than that, right?" Barry asked.

"Yeah, old building. There's a second elevator on fifteen that goes to the other ten floors," said Owen.

They rode the elevator up and exited.

"The second bank is over here," said Owen.

"Shh..."

Everyone froze in place.

"Get into a room, quick!" said Barry, grabbing Kate's hand.

The three of them charged through the first door they saw. It happened to be a dingy supply room with a single bare bulb hanging above. Cleaning supplies lined the shelves. There was hardly any room with the housekeeping cart and mop bucket in there.

The three of them crammed themselves inside and shut the door.

"You better have a good reason for this, Barry," Kate whispered.

"Shh... listen."

At first all Kate could hear was Owen's heavy breathing in her left ear. Then she heard it. The sound of chains being dragged. The sound was getting louder. Whatever was pulling them along, it was getting close to them.

Owen's eyes went wide as he heard footsteps just outside the door. Johnny was right; the creatures from the sewer weren't phantoms. Phantoms wouldn't be making all that noise.

One of the chains smacked against the base of the door. Kate clamped her hand over her mouth to stop herself from screaming. They listened to the metal drag against the length of the door. The creature continued down the hall away from them.

The three of them remained together in the closet like that, amongst the faint smell of bleach, well after they had heard the last of the creature's movements.

Barry cracked the door and peered into the hallway. The coast was clear. He could see impressions in the deep burgundy carpet from where the chains had been dragged.

"Johnny didn't give you any indication what that thing might be?" Barry asked.

"No. Just that there are a ton of them down in the sewers. One chained up at every turn," Owen answered. "And whatever they are, it scared him bad. He said that's how he knows for certain that we're in Hell."

"I don't love the sound of that," said Kate, making her way to the second bank of elevators.

The trio climbed inside the lift and rode it to the observatory. There was a bar and lobby area filled with tables and chairs inside. Like the rest of the place, it was immaculate. Outside, there was a wraparound deck with coin-operated binoculars every five feet.

"Hope one of you brought quarters," said Kate.

"No need. They just work. Just like the diner a block over. You don't need quarters for the jukebox. Nothing in this world needs money to operate, it just works."

"That's how it should be back home, instead of us being nickel and dimed everywhere we go," said Barry.

Owen nodded in agreement.

"Let's split up and each take a different side. Check the tallest buildings. Look for the flash off his binocular's lens."

That's how they spent the next hour.

"Think we should move to another part of the city?" Barry asked.

"Eh, maybe he's not on a rooftop yet. Let's chill in the lobby for a bit and check again," Owen suggested.

"Sounds good, these dogs are barkin'," said Barry.

Barry and Kate went inside and grabbed a table by the window. Barry scooted a chair over and lifted his legs onto the seat. Owen made his way to the bar to check for snacks.

"Don't tell me you guys were out there searching for *me*."

Johnny!

Owen looked behind the bar, but no one was there.

There was a familiar laugh and then, "I'm right here, kid."

Barry sat up with a smile. Kate hopped to her feet.

Owen rounded the wall behind the bar.

What Barry heard next would haunt him for the rest of his life. The sound of Owen struggling to breathe.

A red scaly phantom stepped out from behind the wall.

The mimic.

Its huge, meaty hand was wrapped around Owen's throat.

Owen's feet dangled in the air. He was using all his energy trying to pry the phantom's hand away from his neck.

Barry ran straight at them in time to see the mimic turn its head and smile.

Owen and the phantom both burst into red mist. Only the mist didn't float off as usual. It faded away.

TWELVE

Barry stopped at the exact spot where Owen had disappeared. His head whipped back and forth, frantically searching for some sign of the teenager.

"Barry, what was that? What just happened?"

"I... I don't know."

"Is he... did the phantom..."

Kate couldn't get the words out. She burst into tears.

"Stop it, Kate. It just took him somewhere. I'll find him," said Barry, trying to convince himself as much as he was Kate.

She ran and hugged Barry hard. She mashed her face into his chest.

"Where'd it take him?" she asked.

"I don't know, but I'll find the kid."

Johnny forgotten in the moment, Barry began obsessively searching Palace Plaza for Owen instead. He started in the observatory and made his way all the way down to level three. He opened every single door, every room, every closet, every bathroom stall on every level.

Kate followed slowly behind while he tore the building apart. She had her arms crossed, hugging herself, sniffling between bouts of outright crying. She was positive that Barry wasn't going to find Owen, but she wasn't going to stop him from searching either.

When Barry finally stopped looking, it was only because he had completely lost track of time and night had fallen around them.

He walked to the third story window and looked down at the street below him. A cloaked phantom held out a glowing green lantern in an outstretched hand. It walked the street slowly and swung the spectral light from side to side.

He turned to Kate, finally snapping out of it, and acknowledged that she was there.

"Sorry, I kind of lost myself for a bit there," he whispered.

"It's okay, Barry. Lay down with me. We'll find him in the real world," she told him. "He'll be waiting for us. Either at his house or at your place. I'm sure of it."

Barry surrendered and let Kate lead him by the hand to the bed. They lay down on the cheap hotel mattress and closed their eyes.

When Barry woke, he shook Kate by the shoulder.

"Come on, let's go," he said.

Kate pulled herself out of bed and followed him into the hallway. There was a family just outside their door. A young mother was trying to wrangle a two-year-old while his father slammed the heel of his hand against a wheel on their luggage. They moved past them and took the stairwell down.

The couple rushed out of the plaza and found Kate's vehicle on the street. She drove fast, but not at a completely reckless speed like the day before. It wasn't long before they pulled up outside Owen's house.

There were a lot of cars on the street in front of the home. The driveway was packed full. A few people stood on the lawn talking. A plump woman in a floral dress was crying into a handkerchief on the porch. A thinner woman was beside her, dabbing her eyes with a tissue.

"Oh, no. No, no, no," Barry said, getting out of the car.

Kate rushed through the front lawn and grabbed the back of a young man's arm.

"What happened? Where's Owen?" she asked.

"They already took the body," he answered.

"WHAT? What the fuck are you talking about?" she shouted.

Barry reached her and took hold of her waist. He pulled her a couple of feet back from the guy.

"Oh, sorry. I thought you already knew. Did Aunt Sherry call you?"

"What happened?" Barry asked very sternly.

"Owen hung himself, man. His mom found him this morning in his bedroom."

"Fuck," Barry exclaimed.

Kate screamed. A blood-curdling scream that was heard half a mile away. Everyone's attention was on her.

"He didn't fucking kill himself," she yelled through tears. "It was the phantom! The fucking phantom got him!"

There were murmurs all around them. People started coming out of the house. Barry lifted her and carried her back toward the car. He heard bits of conversation behind him.

"That's that crazy girl that graduated a few years back."

"I bet they met at the mental hospital."

Barry forcefully put Kate in the passenger seat and was about to close the door when two men approached from behind.

"Did she say phantom?" the taller guy asked.

"Sorry about that. She's upset. We both are. We're leaving," said Barry.

"I'm Sam. This is Eric. We went to the phantom realm as well," he said.

Barry stopped what he was doing and turned to examine the pair. Sam was tall, in his early twenties. Eric was short, chubby, and had to be nearly forty.

"Which one of you met him on the other side?" Eric asked.

"Both of us," said Barry.

"You still going through it, or did you close the rift?"

"We're still going through it," Barry answered.

"Holy shit. Are you the guys that Owen helped escape? Johnny told him you were dead," said Kate from the passenger seat.

"Yeah. We didn't know his last name or how to find him. We tried looking him up online. Even waited outside the high school a few times like creeps trying to spot him leaving at dismissal. We knew he'd want to know we made it out safe. Never got the chance to tell him that his plan worked. That he saved our lives. He deserved to know he was a hero."

"How'd you know to come here this morning?" Barry asked with a tear rolling down his cheek.

"The police scanner and a hunch," said Eric. "I was hoping to God it wasn't him. I can't believe they got him."

"Hey! You freaks better get the hell out of here! This ain't no roadside attraction," a man yelled coming toward them from the house.

He tugged his shirt up and let the group see the pistol tucked in his waistband.

"Shit, we need to get out of here," said Barry, jogging around to the driver's seat.

Before he sat down, Barry turned and made eye contact with Sam, who was backing away.

Sam raised his fist and yelled, "Tell Johnny he was wrong about everything. Do what Owen said. Face your demons. Fight your phantom. Fight *your* phantom."

The guy with the gun was getting dangerously close to the car.

"How will I know it's *my* phantom?" Barry called back.

Almost too quietly Sam said, "You'll know."

THIRTEEN

"Barry, this is too much," Kate said, curling into a ball in the passenger seat. "I think I'm going to lose it."

Barry zipped through traffic. His cell phone rang inside the cupholder, but he ignored it.

"This will be our last time going over. We'll end it for good," he told her.

"You don't know that," she said through tears. "We could end up like Owen. Our families are going to think we did it to ourselves."

"Don't say that. We know what's going on now and we know how to stop it."

"Sam said we have to fight *our* phantom. What does that even mean? Which one is ours? How do you even fight one of those things?"

Barry's cell phone rang for the third time. He snatched it from the cupholder and brought it to his ear.

"Hello?"

"Where the hell are you?"

"Excuse me?" Barry asked, with bite in his voice.

"Do you see what time it is? Why aren't you here, Barry?" Mr. Meyers asked.

With everything going on, Barry hadn't even realized it was Monday.

"Sorry, Mr. Meyers, I don't think I can make it in. A close friend of mine just passed away."

"We don't give bereavement for friends. Either get your ass in here or start looking for another job."

"You know what? Fuck you, Peter. I quit."

Barry ended the call. His chest was heaving up and down as he pulled the car into a parking space behind his old pickup truck. Kate had lifted her face from her knees and stared at him with glossy eyes.

"You all right?" she asked.

"Actually, that felt pretty damn good."

They spent the entire day at Barry's apartment, never straying far from one another. Barry wanted to strategize about the day to come but Kate was in rough shape. He didn't want to push her.

Pretty early into the evening, Barry produced an old bottle of melatonin and suggested they get the day over with. Kate nodded in agreement. They chewed up the tablets and crawled into bed.

At 3am, what many people refer to as the "witching hour," the pair slipped to the other side while they slept.

They both sat up suddenly in bed. Someone or something was beating against the apartment's front door.

"What the hell? What is that?" Barry asked.

Kate looked at the clock. It was only 4:32am.

"Did we even cross over?"

"I don't know. Could be a burglar, but I doubt it."

They heard the wood splinter and break apart. Whatever it was, it was getting inside.

"Help me move the bed," Barry shouted.

The two of them pushed the bed across the room and slid it against the bedroom door. Barry knocked his dresser on top of the mattress for good measure. They rushed to put on their clothes.

The smashing stopped. They heard bits of wood clattering to the floor as something made its way inside. Followed by the sound of chains being dragged through the hallway.

A wave of panic pulsed through Barry.

"The window! Go!" he shouted.

The creature began beating against the bedroom door. It held, but it wouldn't for long.

Kate raised the window and climbed onto the slight overhang above the sidewalk. Barry followed her out and then lowered himself over the edge. He dropped to the sidewalk and held out his hands for Kate. She tumbled into his firm arms.

The early morning was silent around them. They knew they had definitely crossed over.

"Hand me your keys," Barry ordered.

Kate froze.

"They're on your kitchen counter," she said just above a whisper.

Barry dug into his pants pocket and found his truck key.

"We're okay. I've got mine. I guess we're just going to have to go loud today," he remarked.

They climbed into Barry's pickup. The engine boomed and the exhaust rattled. The sky was filled with soft blue light. The sun hadn't even come up yet and the hellish day was upon them.

"Where to?" Kate asked.

"We stick to the plan. Find Johnny. Find our phantoms."

Barry raced through town and veered onto the highway.

"We broke the first rule," said Kate. "We stayed at your place two nights in a row. Owen told us not to do that. That's why the phantom found us so fast."

"I don't think it's a phantom."

Kate glared across the seat.

"Then what is it?" she asked.

"I don't know. Phantoms are deadly silent. It would have just traveled through the cracks in the door as smoke and then killed us in our sleep. I think this is from the sewer. You heard the chains, right?"

"The phantom that put the sledgehammer through the wall wasn't silent about it. The mimic's calls aren't silent either," Kate reasoned.

Barry thought for a moment and shrugged.

"You make a good point, I don't know what the hell that thing is. Johnny is going to tell me what he saw down in the sewers though, even if I have to beat it out of him. I need to know what's following me."

Barry got off the exit at full speed and shot through the city of Arlington. The truck's loud exhaust echoed through the empty streets as he took dangerously fast turn after fast turn. Kate held onto the door handle to keep herself from sliding.

"What's the gameplan here? Drive around the city like a maniac?" Kate asked.

"I'm looking for a tall building we haven't been to yet. That's where we'll either find Johnny or be able to scout from. It's the only plan we've got."

Barry took the next turn at too high of a speed. In the middle of the road was one of the cloaked phantoms holding a glowing green lantern. Barry swerved to avoid the creature but overcompensated. The truck popped onto two wheels and then smashed down onto the driver's side of the vehicle. It slid across the road in a shower of sparks and screeching metal.

"Fuck! Why are those things always in the middle of the road?" Barry yelled. "You, okay?"

Kate dangled by her seatbelt above Barry.

"Is it too late to ask you to slow down?" she said with a grin.

She unclipped her seatbelt and fell against Barry. He yelled out in pain.

"What? Are you hurt?" she asked.

"My left foot is pinned. I can't get it free."

"Barry, the phantom! It's coming!"

"Distract it," Barry ordered, frantically pulling on his left ankle with both hands.

Kate kicked out the remainder of the windshield and crawled onto the road. Bits of glass and asphalt dug into the palms of her hands.

She scrambled to her feet and circled to the back of the tipped truck. The phantom glided across the road toward her and abruptly stopped.

Kate watched as the phantom pulled a pocket watch from its cloak and clicked it open. It appeared to check the time before it slowly raised its gnarled hand. Its wrinkled index finger pointed at Kate.

She stood there mesmerized, watching as the green light from the lantern grew brighter and brighter. She raised her forearm to shield her eyes against its blinding radiance.

Suddenly the light blinked out. It took Kate's eyes a moment to adjust in the dim light. The phantom was no longer there. In its place there was a horrible version of Kate herself. Nude, with an oversized head. Its arms were eerily long. All over its body razorblades stuck out from its skin. Each wound wept dark red blood.

It was a version of Kate with all her insecurities overexaggerated.

Kate turned to the truck. Black smoke was billowing out from under the hood.

"Barry," she shouted, "I found my phantom."

The truck seemed to rock slightly but there was no answer from inside.

Kate slowly scanned the ground around her, then sidestepped to her right. The creature mirrored her movement.

She bent at the knees and picked up a large stone.

"You don't frighten me," Kate told the creature. "I'm above all that petty bullshit now."

Barry freed himself from the truck's cab and watched from on top of the wreckage.

The creature stepped forward toward Kate and raised its arms as if asking for a hug. Blood dripped from the cuts and splattered against the road.

Kate let out a scream. No, she let out a battle cry. She surged forward and hurled the heavy rock into the creature's oversized head.

That was all it took. In an instant, both versions of Kate exploded into clouds of gray smoke and faded away.

Barry clenched his fist and whispered, "Atta girl."

He was suddenly startled by the sound of boots thudding against the road behind him.

"Barry, is that you?"

Against all odds, it was Johnny.

Barry laughed. "It sure is. I'm glad to see you. Help me down, will ya? My foot got crushed."

Johnny ran over to the truck and gave Barry his hand.

"Is that sarcastic girl okay? I thought I heard her scream."

Barry laughed again. "Yeah, she's better than okay. But hey, we need to talk."

"I have a house set up down the block. Let's get you some painkillers for that foot."

They started walking down the middle of the street. Barry limped along while smoke drifted into the sky behind him.

"I'm afraid I've got some bad news about Owen."

While they walked, Barry explained what had happened and how they confirmed it in the real world.

"That's where we met Sam and Eric."

Johnny stopped walking and turned to Barry.

"They're alive?"

"Owen's theory was right. You have to face your phantom. It's how you get out of this place."

"Maybe you can. I told you before, it's a different situation for me. I'm dead. This is my Hell."

Barry put his hand on Johnny's shoulder.

"You have to listen to me when I say this, Johnny. That's not true. Owen took us to your hospital room.

You're in a coma and I think you can wake back up. There's still time."

Just as the wave of shock passed over Johnny's face, they heard chains being dragged through the streets. Up ahead, something was coming.

Johnny stepped back away from the sound. There was terror in his eyes like nothing Barry had ever seen before.

"What is that? What did you see down in the sewers?"

"You don't want to know. You just need to run."

"No, Johnny. I need to know, and we have to stop running. It's time to go home."

"My family," Johnny said softly. "I was at work. The power went out. There was a problem with our generator. The house filled with carbon monoxide. They all died while I sat at my computer five miles away."

The sound of chains grew louder. Whatever was coming was almost on them.

"When I went down into the sewer, they were all chained up down there, Barry. My wife. My children. Their eyes were as black as coal, and they wanted my blood."

A small boy rounded the corner dragging two long lengths of chain behind him. Only it was Barry who reacted, not Johnny. Barry fell to his knees.

In the mall, at the plaza, back at the apartment, this is what he had heard.

"NOOOO!" Barry wailed.

Jay looked the same as the last time Barry had seen him, dead on the road. A sickly pale color to him, blood caked on one ear. Only now his eyes were jet black.

Jay moved closer to Barry.

"Who is it?" Johnny asked.

"My little brother," Barry said through tears.

Johnny's chest rose and fell with deep breaths. You could see his mind at work.

"No! No, it's not, Barry. I was wrong about everything. That's a phantom!"

Jay was just eight feet in front of Barry now, who was still on his knees. His arms hung by his sides in defeat.

Jay took another step closer.

"Not just a phantom. *Your* phantom. And it's taking the shape of your baby brother to hurt you. Are you going to fall into its trap?"

Barry raised his head.

"Are you going to let it steal his image? Are you going to let it disgrace your brother's memory?"

Barry slapped the ground hard with both hands and rose to his feet.

"Fuck no," he said and charged at the creature.

Barry barreled into the child-sized phantom. His meaty shoulder smacked into its frail chest.

They both exploded into a cloud of gray mist.

FOURTEEN

The following Saturday, Barry and Kate met up with Sam and Eric at the Orchard Bay Cemetery. Owen's family had a private service and a private burial, but the four of them still attended. It was just at a respectful distance away.

They watched as the casket was lowered into the ground from a hill overlooking the plot. A freezing wind blew at their backs. They couldn't hear the words from the priest but they shed tears all the same.

When the family had departed, the four of them walked through the field of graves. Barry walked with a limp, an air cast covering his left foot. When they reached Owen's burial place, each dropped a single rose onto the lowered casket. They hugged each other. They cried. They remembered all that the kid had done for them. He was a hero to them all.

The moment was interrupted by the sound of a vehicle coming their way. Barry and the others turned to watch as it circled the cemetery and pulled up alongside them. They were surprised to see it was a medical transport van.

The driver circled around to drop the wheelchair ramp and then climbed inside.

Kate's eyes grew wide as the realization hit her. All three guys wore satisfied smiles as they watched Johnny come out to join them.

EPILOGUE

After Barry closed the rift between worlds, life had gotten better.

Friendship blossomed with Eric, Sam, and Johnny. They met up twice a month for a poker game. Barry mostly lost but they never played high stakes.

Barry found a new job, working as a grief counselor of all things. He was mindful to look for signs that his clients may be passing through the rift.

He moved in with Kate, and their relationship grew strong.

Barry stopped seeing his therapist and was taking real joy in all the little things again. Kate still saw hers, but she was like an all-new person these days.

Barry had heard Peter Meyers was fired for stealing money. They had found missing bills inside a raincoat in his office. Turns out, someone had anonymously called the corporate office and tipped them off.

Everything had fallen into place and life was just about perfect.

Well, until the episodes started.

His doctor called it sleep paralysis. It's when you regain consciousness after sleeping, but your body is unable to move and you're unable to speak. You're basically paralyzed but awake.

Barry's doctor laughed when he told him that some people even claim to see demons in that state.

Barry didn't laugh.

Kate suggested they weren't really there. He was just in his dream state, and he should use it as a reminder to stay on his healthy path.

Barry disagreed. He didn't believe he was dreaming.

Each time it happened, it was a different phantom. He'd wake to find them at the foot of the bed, just standing there. Then they'd slowly circle around to his side of the bed. Some of them would even lean down so they were face to face with him. Barry could feel their hot breath against his skin.

It didn't feel like a reminder. It didn't feel like a warning. It felt like a threat.

Dear Reader,

I appreciate your support with my books tremendously. If you enjoyed the book and you'd like to help me further, please consider leaving a rating or review. Either one of those on Amazon or Goodreads will help others find and select my books for purchase. That small act would mean the world to me. Thank you!

-Dylan

If you or someone you know is struggling with mental health, please know that you are not alone. Help is available.

For immediate support in the United States:
Call or text 988 — the **Suicide & Crisis Lifeline**
Available 24/7, free, and confidential.

For more mental health resources, visit:
988lifeline.org

Your mental health matters. Please reach out.

Other books by Dylan Gibbs

Night Terrors
A Collection of Short Stories

From the Woods
A Collection of Short Stories

Demon Twins
(Book of Demons #1)
A Novel

Demon Blade
(Book of Demons #2)
A Novel

Summer of Shadows
A Novel

Dylan Gibbs is from a small town in Central New York. He is a family man first and foremost. He has a wonderful wife and three beautiful children. Although he works a blue-collar job, he's spent his adulthood writing stories. Dylan has always been curious about the things that frighten us most. His writing style is primarily geared for young adult readers but anyone with a love of horror and thriller genres will enjoy. He has plans for several future publications.

Made in the USA
Middletown, DE
07 October 2025